"Get o[f...]"

The voice—deep and [...] them. Jamie squinted [...] side of the road. The man staring down at her [...] look anything like the sleek, power-suited young oil-and-gas executive in the old news clippings. The man up on that cliff looked...rough...wild...and *very* angry.

Jamie shaded her eyes with a shaky hand. "Hello, Mr. Biddle, I'm—"

"I have my detectives, Ms. Evans. I know all about you."

"Of course you do." *How much did he know?*

"Isn't the story of my wife's disappearance too old for you media types?"

Jamie's uneasiness intensified. He wasn't reacting like a man in shock, a man who'd just been given terrible news. *But surely the authorities had contacted him.* Suddenly Jamie, who could spew out snappy lines for the camera without preparation, was having trouble finding words.

"Mr. Biddle, a source informed me an hour ago that...that your wife's...her remains were found this morning. I'm...I'm sorry."

For one moment Nathan Biddle sat so still atop his horse that he looked like a statue. He didn't seem to be breathing. Then he turned the horse and headed back the way he'd come.

Jamie, despite her gift for glibness, could only stare at him soundlessly.

Dear Reader,

Trust your instincts. We've all heard that expression, but for Jamie Evans and Nathan Biddle it's an especially tall order. They have every reason to *mistrust* each other. Early in my research, I became enthralled with this idea of trust. I had traveled to the heart of the Osage Hills and heard tales of ancient betrayals that haunted me for days.

Shortly after that trip, I was delighted when Oklahoma's gracious First Lady, Cathy Keating, invited me to join her for lunch at the governor's mansion. Mrs. Keating, herself a published author, loves books—those by Oklahomans in particular. She had obtained a copy of my Superromance novel, *The Pull of the Moon*, set in Tulsa, and she wanted to visit about the writing life. We talked about the great synergy of culture and history that makes Oklahoma unique—real cowboys, proud Indians, wild outlaws, wealthy oil barons. When I told Cathy that I was working on a story set on a ranch in the Osage Hills near the Tallgrass Prairie Preserve, her eyes lit up.

For the next hour we bubbled with conversation about the deep forested canyons, the endless lakes and lush rolling hills of northeastern Oklahoma. Cathy fired up my imagination with lore about the historic town of Pawhuska and the Osage tribe, who became the wealthiest people per capita in the United States during the early oil boom days.

It is against this backdrop that Jamie Evans and Nathan Biddle not only learn to trust their instincts and believe in each other…they learn what it means to fall deeply in love.

I always enjoy hearing from my readers. Visit my Web site at http://www.superauthors.com or write to me at P.O. Box 720224, Norman, OK 73070.

Darlene Graham

The Man from Oklahoma
Darlene Graham

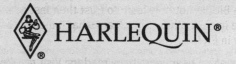

HARLEQUIN®

TORONTO • NEW YORK • LONDON
AMSTERDAM • PARIS • SYDNEY • HAMBURG
STOCKHOLM • ATHENS • TOKYO • MILAN • MADRID
PRAGUE • WARSAW • BUDAPEST • AUCKLAND

ISBN 0-373-70994-3

THE MAN FROM OKLAHOMA

Copyright © 2001 by Darlene Gardenhire.

Visit us at www.eHarlequin.com

Printed in U.S.A.

To my beloved brothers, Ron and Rick.

You two have known me since the days of the dugout
in the pasture and "The Claw."
Amazingly, you still believe in me.

PROLOGUE

AT ELEVEN-THIRTY on an ordinary Wednesday morning, right smack in the middle of his workweek, Susie Biddle called her husband Nathan's office, and after making sure he wasn't on the speakerphone or some such thing, informed him in a teasing voice that she was wearing "that little black thing," and would he, perhaps, be interested in running home for lunch?

Nathan, after picking up the chair he'd tipped over, beat a path past his secretary's desk and told her in a false-sounding too-loud voice that his wife had taken ill suddenly, and that he had to rush home immediately to tend to her. Cancel this afternoon's meeting.

On his way out—sans coat, tie or briefcase—a couple of the secretaries in the outer office cast knowing smiles at each other, as if they suspected his real mission. Had Susie discussed their infertility troubles with these women? The thought might have bothered him under other circumstances, but, Nathan asked himself, considering the current state of their marriage, did he care? No, he most certainly did not.

Susie opened the door of their fine old Tulsa home before he even got the key in the lock. Sure enough, there she stood, with a come-hither look on her face and one hand planted saucily on her hip, wearing only that little black thing.

Man.

Nathan Biddle hadn't seen the little black thing—or a willing wife—in quite a long time.

"Well?" was all she said.

With one big hand at her tiny waist and the other grasping the back of her slender neck, Nathan pulled Susie against his body while he danced her backward, toward privacy, all the while giving her a lusty kiss.

"You crazy woman," he growled when they got to the door of the master suite. Then he kissed her again. Fiercely. Joyously. For at last the clouds of discontent that had enveloped her these past months seemed to have parted.

"Not crazy," Susie said, laughing as his hungry mouth made its way down her slender neck. "Just fertile."

But Nathan—who had never in their entire ten-year marriage received a call that tantalizing from Susie, fertile or not—was way beyond caring about Susie's endless obsession with calendars and basal thermometers and fertility charts. Right now all he wanted was Susie.

She smelled like pure heaven and her skin felt as soft as rose petals. Her answering kisses told him that this was going to be easy, so easy. He didn't feel even a glimmer of the anxiety about pregnancy that had disabled their sex life in recent months.

In fact, on that Wednesday afternoon, Nathan Biddle didn't feel anything at all except Susie. Only Susie.

CHAPTER ONE

Oh, most beautiful of women,
You will wear the white of happiness.
My soul will slide into your soul.
I could never be lonely when I am with you.
  —from an ancient Native American song
                        to attract affection

Three years later

"IN THE VALLEY behind me, you can see the Hart Ranch, home of Tulsa philanthropist, Nathan Biddle. Biddle, known for his many efforts on behalf of disadvantaged children, has been living as a recluse in his childhood home here in these Osage Hills for three years, ever since his wife, oil heiress Susan Claremont Biddle, disappeared. But early this morning, authorities— Dammit!" Jamie Evans lowered her hand mike and tossed a hank of honey-blond hair out of her eyes. "The wind up here is absolutely ridiculous! Sorry, Dave. We'll have to reshoot."

Jamie sighed as she tottered across the gravel

road on high heels toward the Channel Six van, wondering why she'd spent so much energy convincing her news director they needed this footage. All this work, all this setup, for ten seconds of film that would be obsolete by eleven o'clock tonight. But her instincts told her that this time she was on to something big. There was more to this story than a missing oil heiress whose remains had finally been found. As if that wasn't enough. But the strange way Nathan Biddle had kept himself hidden in these hills, completely cut off from his former life only an hour away in Tulsa...

"You know, maybe we should forget about shooting from this plateau." The lanky young cameraman tugged at his earring and made a disgruntled face at the forbidding isolated terrain below. "Aren't we trespassing?"

Jamie glanced over her shoulder. Why was Dave so edgy? The ink was barely dry on his degree, but Dave Reardon was normally as aggressive as the most seasoned photojournalist. "Trespassing? On a ranch this big? Come on," she chided, "look at that view—the meanders of the river and everything. You can see the entire ranching complex." She fanned an arm toward the buildings below: a two-story native-sandstone house with a plantation-style porch stretching across its front; two long modern steel horse barns; and an old-fashioned gambrel-roofed barn, complete with a charming hay door tucked under the peak. Hart Ranch was a venerable old establishment, dating back to territorial days.

"That's one fantastic visual." She turned and made a face at her reflection in the side mirror of the Channel Six van. "Everybody wants to know what Biddle's ranch looks like—especially now. I'm telling you, this'll make a terrific teaser." She yanked the door open, grabbing a brush and a can of hairspray off the front seat.

"None of the other stations have time to get out here and back to Tulsa before the newscast. They'll all run the same old head shot of our ugly DA, preening and posturing about solving this heinous crime."

She made a couple of determined chops at her thick hair, then stopped. "Wonder if I can show a close-up of the mysterious Mr. Biddle's face at ten o'clock? By then they might have the dental records matched, maybe even know the cause of death, and I'll have my second source confirmed, et cetera, et cetera."

Dave was studying the landscape through the camera lens. "Dream on," he muttered. "Nobody's caught him on film for at least two years." He lowered the camera. "Unless you're gonna pull a Jamie and go banging on his front door or something."

"I might." Banging on the door was exactly

what she would do in most cases. But this wasn't like most cases. She knew the Biddles' story too well. This man would undoubtedly be in shock, in pain.

"I've got to think that one through." She gave her hair one last swipe and started spraying. "Man! How on earth can a place be this windy and still be so warm in the middle of October?"

Her panty hose were sticking to her legs like plastic wrap, and her cream-colored linen suit couldn't be more wrinkled if she'd slept in it. She'd probably look like holy hell on camera. *But, hey, that's life.* Jamie had been working on this story ever since she transferred to Tulsa from Kansas City, and she wasn't about to blow an opportunity like this—a one-of-a-kind six-o'clock teaser about the biggest breaking story in ages.

Her only regret was that she hadn't come out to the ranch to sneak this footage before now. But who would have imagined the body would be found way out here in Osage County? It sure paid to have sources in the DA's office. Still not satisfied with her hair repairs, she gave up and glanced back at Dave.

"Who would actually choose to live out in the middle of this godforsaken prairie?" She tossed the hairspray back onto the front seat.

Dave shrugged. "A guy whose family has owned the place since before the Land Run, I guess.'' He went back to studying the view through the lens.

Dave had done his homework, too. They were a great team, charging around the state scooping the competition on stories that were visually startling and chock-full of eyewitness accounts and pithy little sound bites. They were so good that Dave's footage and Jamie's voice-over had once been picked up by the network news.

Only four years out of journalism school, pretty as a peach and smart as a whip, Jamie Evans was the undisputed princess of Channel Six, the one who garnered all the awards. The one the viewer focus groups liked most. The one people phoned the station to gush about.

And call it luck or call it instinct, but Jamie Evans was also the reporter who managed to be in the right place at the right time.

''Hey!'' Dave cried. ''I think I spotted our man!''

''Get a shot! Get a close-up!'' Jamie ran across the road as fast as she dared in the heels.

Dave was already filming.

''Zoom in on his face,'' Jamie urged. She tiptoed at Dave's side but couldn't see much without the magnification of the camera lens. ''It's got to be Biddle. He lives out here all alone.'' She peered down at the ranch house, the outbuildings and the corrals below as the thrill of the chase coursed

through her. "Try to get a good clean close-up."
Her heart pounded when she spotted a big man in
a cowboy hat emerging from the barn with a horse
on a lead.

"Uh-oh." The skinny photographer jerked back
from the lens. "He spotted us, too." He frowned
as he refocused. "Man! That dude looks mean."

"Lemme look."

Dave held the camera steady while Jamie
scanned the scene below.

"Where the hell is he?"

Dave adjusted the camera upward and the man
came into focus. Jamie almost stumbled off her
high heels at the sight of him.

He was mounting a big muscular paint, and as
Jamie watched his movements, her throat went dry.
He was long-legged, broad-shouldered, wearing
tight jeans, a faded chambray shirt and a beatup
black cowboy hat.

He pulled the horse's head around and took off
at a hard gallop toward a dirt road that disappeared
into a stand of blackjacks. Jamie figured—*feared*—
that the road led to this plateau.

And when he got here, he would run them off.
Great.

"Dave, he's coming. You have the red light disabled?"

"Always," Dave said. He was already taking
the camera off the tripod.

"Okay. Whatever he says, whatever he does, keep that camera rolling. Aimed at *him*."

Dave made a face that said *duh*. "You really think I should film this guy?" he said, "I was thinking it'd be better to get a good clean close-up of these rocks."

Jamie ignored him and chewed a nail, thinking. "And don't be obvious about it."

"Huh?" Dave's sarcasm was replaced by genuine confusion. Normally the photographer rolled the camera openly while Jamie let fly a barrage of questions.

"We're out here all alone," Jamie explained.

Dave winced and tugged on his earring. "So I noticed."

Shoving her misbehaving hair firmly behind one ear, Jamie took a deep breath and walked with Dave to the edge of the plateau where they stood in plain sight, looking like a couple of stranded motorists. Jamie checked behind her, down the sloping gravel road. "You're sure he saw us?" she asked after a few uncomfortable minutes had passed with no sign of the rider.

"Yeah. Look, the wind's picking up and the sun's getting low. Wanna try to finish shooting the teaser?"

Jamie sighed. "Why not? At least we'll look like we know what we're doing." She stood in her former spot, faced the camera and started to talk.

"This is Jamie Evans, and behind me you see the Hart Ranch complex, home of Tulsa oil tycoon Nathan Hart Biddle—"

"Get off my land." The voice—deep, powerful and sure—had come from above them. Jamie squinted up the wall of a rocky cliff on the other side of the road. With the sun behind him he stood out clearly, a striking silhouette among the black shapes of low cedars. The curves of his hat, the ragged tail of his hair blowing in the wind, the profile of the paint, all blended into a haunting image that made Jamie shudder.

The steely-eyed raven-haired man looking down at her seemed eerily familiar. Jamie chalked up the sensation to the fact that she had been studying archival news photos of the Biddles for the past couple of years. His face had surely been burned into her subconscious by now. But the Nathan Biddle staring down at her didn't look anything like the sleek power-suited young oil-and-gas executive in those old news photos. The man up on that cliff looked...rough...wild, more like the aged sepia photographs she'd found of his Osage great-grandfather, Chief Black Wing.

She shaded her eyes with a shaky hand. "Hello. I'm Jamie Ev—"

"I know who you are. Isn't this story getting a bit shopworn for your kind?"

Her kind? Well, she'd resent reporters, too, if

she'd gone through what this man had. The media had insisted on going for the dramatic tear-jerker angle, focusing on the Biddles' high-profile marriage— God, that must have been awful for him. Jamie began to feel sorry for the man.

"Could we talk to you, Mr. Biddle?"

"No. You are trespassing. Now leave."

Jamie's uneasiness intensified. He wasn't acting like a man in shock, a man who'd just been given terrible news. *But surely the authorities had already contacted him.*

"Mr. Biddle, you really don't know why we're out here this afternoon?" She shot Dave a look and saw that the tape was rolling, though he had the camera braced casually under one arm.

The horse nickered in the answering silence. Then Biddle turned the animal and disappeared into the sun's rays.

"What now?" Dave whispered.

"Just keep rolling."

In no time horse and rider appeared around the base of the cliff. Man and animal seemed to move as one unit as they maneuvered expertly around leafless saplings and belly-high bluestem grass. In the saddle, Nathan Biddle looked relaxed, but his intense dark eyes remained fixed warily on Jamie as he rode toward her. Nobody said a word, so that as he reined the horse in, the squeak of leather and the crunch of gravel seemed magnified.

He stayed in the saddle, high above them. "Turn it off," he said to Dave without looking at him. Dave made elaborate motions as if doing so.

"Talk," Biddle said to Jamie while he gave her a once-over that made her want to run and crouch behind a limestone boulder. The close proximity of the massive horse didn't help. Jamie had always been scared of horses.

"I'm sorry, Mr. Biddle," she started, "we didn't mean to disturb you. I work for Channel Six, as you know, and we've been following your story for some time—"

"I have my detectives, Ms. Evans. I know all about you."

"Of course you do." *So how much do you know?*

"Get to the point."

Jamie swallowed and started again. "We're shooting a teaser—I'm planning to do a package on the ten-o'clock news and—"

"A package? Why?"

It didn't surprise her that he knew the terminology for a feature-length TV news story. "Why?" Jamie's throat went dry.

His dark eyes narrowed at her hesitation. "The story of my wife's disappearance is old, Ms. Evans. It's…dead."

"Well, uh, that's just it. Something's happened,

I'm afraid. The authorities haven't contacted you?''

''About what?''

''I don't know how to tell you this.''

Biddle didn't move.

''I don't have any details, but...'' Jamie, who could spew out lines for a snappy stand-up shot with no preparation, was having trouble finding words.

''What is this about?'' Biddle demanded.

''Mr. Biddle, a source informed me about an hour ago that...that your wife's...her remains were found this morning. By hunters. I'm...I'm sorry.'' Jamie's voice grew weak and the last word had come out almost soundless.

For one moment Nathan Biddle sat so still atop the paint that he looked like a statue. He didn't even seem to be breathing. Then he closed his eyes, swallowed and drew in a tortured breath. ''Where?'' he said through tightened lips.

''On a sandbar, a small island, out in the Arkansas River,'' Jamie answered softly.

Biddle did not turn his head, but his eyes moved to the camera. ''Use any of that—'' he angled the hat subtly toward Dave ''—and I will sue your asses off.''

Dave slid his fingers around and pressed the off button on the camera, this time for real.

Biddle turned the paint, heading back the way

he had come. This time the squeak of leather and the crunch of gravel made an eerie counterpoint to the fading light and gusting evening air. He didn't look back as he galloped across the road, up the embankment and around the rocky base of the cliff.

Jamie, with her gift for glibness, could only stare at his back as he rode away, unable to think of a thing to say. But what could one possibly say to a man who had just been told that after three long years, his wife's remains had been found in this wild lonely country?

"I promise," she finally murmured, "I won't use the footage." But Dave was the only one who heard her.

CHAPTER TWO

ALONE. THE WORD took on a new and terrible meaning as Nathan Biddle stared out at the spectacular sunset he had seen so many times from this broad window. He braced his palms wide on the sill, suddenly remembering the day his grandfather Biddle had installed the majestic expanse of glass in the western wall of the enormous Hart Ranch house.

"Nathan, my boy," the old man had said, "your grandmother's people came from those hills out there. The Osage, a fierce and proud nation. And filthy rich, too!" Gramps had slapped him on the back as if it was a great joke.

For so long—months after Susie had disappeared—Nathan had waited for a ransom note that never came. Maybe someone was after the Osage oil money, he and his lawyers had reasoned. Such atrocities, in the name of greed, had been visited upon the wealthy Osage people before. Nathan hoped that maybe someone would demand the millions that he would gladly pay, and then Susie and their unborn child would be magically restored to him.

But now these Osage Hills, beloved resting place, of his ancestors, had become Susie's resting place, as well. She had been out there all this time. All this time while he had been searching the world for her, she had been right out there on an island in a river...*alone.*

He had sensed from the first, of course, that Susie would never come back. Had felt it in his body.

Hunters, the reporter woman had said. He hadn't even turned on the TV. And wouldn't. He did not want to see what the jackals were saying about Susie, about him, about the one who had done this. That was for the city people in Tulsa to look at, to eat with their nightly meal, digesting someone else's pain like so much junk food. Tears stung his eyes.

The clouds gathered in radiant silence as the liquid orange Oklahoma sun touched down on the rim of the rolling hills. Nathan focused his burning eyes there, at that convergence of light on the far horizon.

He tried not to think of the last time he had seen Susie, but her voice reverberated in his mind, anyway: *"Nathan, I'm pregnant!"* Those words would echo in him forever, like his own heartbeat. They had been the words he'd desperately wanted to hear, though he'd never admitted it, not to her, not even to himself.

Their battle against infertility, the child they were finally going to have, none of it seemed real now. It seemed as if the only thing that remained from his former life was this land where he had grown up, these endless hills.

He put his forehead to the glass and fought the rage, the tears, the self-pity. When his mind cooled and he raised his head, the clouds seemed brighter than any he had ever seen. The strange sight caused a sudden unease to pass over him. He looked around the room, cast in an amber glow, and the furniture—his grandfather's furniture— looked the same as it always had, yet not the same at all.

Grief, he knew by now, could have strange and unpredictable effects on a man's mind. He turned his head slowly, looking back at the clouds, and they had altered again. Before his eyes they suddenly took shape above the setting sun as first one, then many faces formed. As he stared, this wall of faces stirred in him an unbidden anger, then sadness and finally a strange resolve. It seemed as if this vision had been trying to form for the past three years. He shook his head and blinked, then rubbed his eyes. When he looked again, the faces had vanished. Only ordinary clouds remained, following the sun to bed.

He turned from the window and the room looked ordinary again, too. Like the same old place where the same evening sun had shone in the same way ever since he was a small boy.

He stumbled to the wide leather couch facing the fireplace and sprawled on his back, suddenly stricken with a blinding headache.

Which was where his cousin Robert found him.

"Nathan!" Robert yelled as he crashed through the front door, then halted abruptly when he caught sight of the figure on the couch with one arm flung over his eyes.

"Nathan," Robert repeated more quietly, and Nathan heard his cousin's boots clomp heavily as he crossed the hardwood floor. Nathan sensed Robert standing over him. "Are you all right? I came here as soon as I heard the television reports."

Nathan lowered his arm.

Six and a half feet tall, thick-necked and thick-middled, with a tail of unkempt jet-black hair trailing down his back, Robert Hart looked like nothing so much as a sorrowful young bull, peering down at Nathan. He removed his well-worn baseball cap and held it in both hands. "They said they found her...her bones out there." Robert inclined his head toward the massive window.

Nathan sat up. "Damn the media—reporting it before I've been officially notified."

"So how'd you know?"

"Long story. A reporter." He braced his elbows on his knees and pressed steepled fingers to his lips. "What are the news reports saying?"

Robert sat down next to him. "They said they made a provisional identification," he answered quietly, "by her jewelry."

Nathan nodded. "The Claremont ring. I can imagine what Wanda and Fred are feeling."

Thinking about Susie's mother and father tore at Nathan's heart. He didn't mention his own parents, although he suspected that Robert was picturing them now. Nathan wondered if his cousin was grateful, as he himself was, that Clare and Drew Biddle were not alive to witness this sorrow. Despite Robert's hokey Indian ways, Nathan was suddenly thankful to have this particular man at his side for the ordeal ahead. Robert was a guy you could count on. The cousins were men of one accord, though they lived in different worlds, believed in different things.

"Nathan, don't you want to turn on the TV so you can see for yourself what they're saying?" Robert offered.

No, he did not. But to satisfy Robert, he said, "Okay. Put it on Channel Six." He was, in fact, curious to know if Jamie Evans had used the footage of him. It would feel good to have some petty reason to get righteously angry right now.

Robert got up and opened the doors of the massive armoire and pushed the buttons on a big-screen set. He returned with the remote and handed it to Nathan. A weatherman was talking, pointing at scrolling satellite images of clouds.

"Switch to another channel," Robert suggested. "Maybe one of the other stations has something about it."

"No. I want Channel Six."

"Why Six?"

"Jamie Evans was out here today. She and her photographer. I told them not to use the tape they shot."

"Jamie Evans? That little blond reporter? She was out here on the ranch?"

"If you'd get your head out of your Wordsworth and Shakespeare and step foot out of that rotting old cabin once in a while, you'd know these things, cousin. I spotted them up on the north plateau a little over an hour ago."

"And coming up at ten o'clock," the news anchor was talking again, "complete details on the discovery of the body of missing oil heiress Susan Claremont Biddle. Jamie Evans has more on this late-breaking story. Jamie?"

A stunning strong intelligent young face filled the screen. "Authorities aren't telling us much right now, Nick, but apparently they have reason to believe the remains found by hunters this morning belong to Susan Claremont Biddle. Mrs. Biddle was the twenty-eight-year-old granddaughter of well-known Tulsa oilman Ross Claremont and the wife of Tulsa philanthropist Nathan Hart Biddle. Authorities are awaiting positive identification from dental records.''

The blond woman holding the mike had a creamy complexion and amber-green eyes that caught fire when the studio lights reflected in their depths, then narrowed with reined-in emotion as she spoke. Her perfect full mouth, set in a square jaw, moved with precision over every word. She had the ideal media face, Nathan thought with detachment, a classic movie-star face. Sincere. Appealing. Unforgettable.

''The remains were found by black-powder deer hunters who told authorities they thought they had stumbled on a deer scrape on a sandbar in the Arkansas River. But what they found was the victim's shallow grave. The state medical examiner's office has not released cause-of-death information, but we hope to have more details at ten, as well as a statement from Tulsa County District Attorney Trent Van Horn about the status of this shocking case.''

Nathan hit the mute button and they watched the attractive young reporter mouthing her sign off.

''She's in the studio,'' Nathan mumbled. ''The footage I'm looking for was shot out here in the open. She said it was a teaser, so I guess we missed it. I'd like to know what she showed."

"What's the deal with her?"

"She's an up-and-coming little reporter who's been digging around ever since she came to town. She's young, smart, ambitious. Hot after the sensational crime story that will boost her career."

"Your private investigator can probably find out if she used that footage of you. Although I kinda wonder about old Frank. Goes by the book too much for a private dick, if you ask me. Why hasn't *he* called?"

"He may not know they found her." Nathan's voice was emotionless. "The sheriff doesn't notify the suspect's private detective."

Robert sat stone still for a moment before he slowly nodded. "Suspect. That occurred to me, too, when I was flying down the ridge on my bike. I didn't see any cars around your house, and I thought, what if they haven't contacted Nathan yet because…well…you know…"

"Because they think I killed her?"

Robert turned his head and let his sympathetic brown eyes speak for a moment before he said, "You are in danger, cousin, and you need powerful help."

Nathan studied Robert's serious expression and, despite his emotional turmoil, felt his face pulling into a crooked smile. "Robert, my man, don't even think about that."

"Just talk to him. Or come away with me for a few days. So we can plan, so we can think."

"Talk to your crazy medicine man so he can blow on my face and make me invisible or something?"

"Mr. Elliott has the power to help you. I'm not asking you to go up there and stay forever. Just long enough to prepare yourself. If you went into hiding for a while, we might even have a half a chance of finding the real killer."

"Be sensible, Robert."

"Nathan, *you* be sensible. Van Horn hasn't believed your story from the start. If he doesn't get a conviction, he could lose the election next spring, and you're the only suspect he's got. Is that what you want? To go to prison, to *die,* for something you didn't do? How does that help Susie? If we seek guidance from the shaman—"

"I'll fight this battle my own way. I don't need some old Indian guy singing chants and rattling turtle shells." Nathan shifted and reached for the portable phone on the marble table in front of them. "I'd better call Frank." His private detective was going to be less than thrilled to learn that his missing-person case had turned into a murder investigation. Frank was a sharp old dog, but he was about ready to retire. He wouldn't like taking on something this complicated.

Robert threw up his hands, then stood. "Let me call him. But first let me get you some water. You look like hammered buffalo dung."

"Bring some aspirin, too," Nathan said. "I've got a killer headache. But don't blow on 'em," he added without looking up at his cousin.

Robert glanced back and said, "Humph," before he disappeared behind the stairs, down the long hallway toward the kitchen.

Nathan eased his pounding head back onto the couch and stared up at the high cedar-beamed ceiling. For three years he'd been living with this nightmare. Would it never end? He thought about what lay ahead and the dark crossbeams above him blurred. But a steel-hard resolve quickly cleared his vision. He no longer cared about the ambitions of political phonies in Tulsa, about society's judgment, their courts, their reporters. He no longer cared about anything at all except finding Susie's murderer.

All along his gut had told him that Susie would never be found alive. And now he would probably be charged with her murder. A sensational suspect for a sensational crime.

JAMIE COULDN'T SHAKE OFF the haunting image of Nathan Biddle's face when she'd told him about his wife. As soon as the news crew cleared out after the six-o'clock broadcast, she grabbed the sleeve of Dave's faded flannel shirt. "You're not going anywhere."

"Ah, man!" Dave whined and bounced backward on one sneaker. "Give me a break, lady. Just because you live, eat and breathe this crap doesn't mean I have to. I have a life, you know."

"I need you more than the boys at the Apocalypse Club. Come back to the archives and help me locate an old video of Nathan Biddle. The one on the horse."

"You mean the stuff I shot at that fancy golf tournament for children's medical research?"

"Correct."

"I know exactly where that one is." Dave bit at the challenge. "Follow me." He set off with long lanky strides down the narrow corridor that led toward the editing bay.

The room, no bigger than a closet, was arranged like a command module: two Beta tape decks canted on the desk, two monitors angled inward on the shelf above. Dave took the chair without asking and popped in the tape he'd retrieved. Jamie hovered behind him.

He didn't take long to locate the footage of Nathan Biddle sitting atop a horse in a white cowboy hat and western-style tuxedo, looking like the man who had everything.

"This what you want?" Dave asked as he toggled doorknob-size dials back and forth, cutting and moving footage to the blank tape in the other Beta deck. "I remembered exactly when I shot this, because how many people would think of using a horse, instead of a golf cart?" A close-up shot of Biddle resting his five iron across the saddle horn zoomed forward on the screen. Dave twisted the knobs again. "This kind of work will be a lot easier to do when we get the new AVID system," he said. "We'll be able to do enhancements, pull out nat sound, do perfect lay-downs, everything."

More interested in her subject than the technology Dave adored, Jamie commented softly, "Biddle would pull any stunt to get publicity for his charities."

"Man, his looks sure have changed." Dave brought the face on the screen into sharper focus. "Doesn't even look like the same dude."

"Okay. You can go play now."

Dave got up and gave Jamie the chair, but then he hovered at Jamie's shoulder and studied the viewer as she froze a frame showing a young woman smiling in the background.

"Biddle's wife," Dave said, and Jamie nodded. "Film often catches things you miss in real time."

They watched while the pale-skinned brunette

beauty glanced over her shoulder at someone in the crowd. When she turned back toward the camera, she looked pensive, biting her perfect lower lip.

After a gravid silence, Dave said. "God, she's pretty. You think he did it?"

Jamie sank back in her chair, hypnotized by the image before her. Susan Biddle had indeed been a pretty woman. "Go get me everything else we've got, okay?"

"Jamie, come on. You've seen it all a dozen times."

"Well, I want to see it again, okay? Now go."

Dave bounded away.

Jamie transferred the segment with the wife onto the new tape, then loaded a different cartridge into the first tape deck. This was tonight's video. The one she didn't use. She fast-forwarded past the parts of herself in a fright wig and came to Biddle's face. Just like in the golf segment, he looked down from high up in a saddle. But Dave was right. He did look different. It wasn't just the ranch clothes and the fact that he'd let his hair grow out. His Native American blood seemed to stand out now. In the lines of his face she could see shadows of the Osage warrior depicted in the famous George Catlin painting. The same high forehead, wide mouth, prominent nose. But mostly it was his deep-set eyes that seemed changed, transformed, *revealed.* Handsome and energetic in the older video, they looked darker now, more still. The quiet bottomless eyes of a man who had suffered too much. Even so, something about his face radiated such strength, such compassion, such integrity that Jamie's instincts told her this was a man who could never murder anyone, much less his wife.

Again she watched the reaction that Dave had surreptitiously captured. The shocked realization that passed over the whole man when she told him Susan Biddle's remains had been found. Nobody could fake that. Could they?

She froze the frame and her stomach tightened as she relived that first encounter. It had been so long since she'd been genuinely attracted to a man that she'd just about given up. Her big sister, Valerie, oh-so-happily married and busy making babies with a nice ordinary mechanical engineer in Kansas City, claimed Jamie had some kind of complex about bad boys. Valerie would never let Jamie forget her disastrous post-high-school fling with a motorcycle-riding wild guy named Ethan.

Could she help it, Jamie had argued the last time they'd talked about men, if she couldn't imagine kissing ninety-nine percent of the nice guys she met, much less being married to one of them? But when she imagined kissing Nathan Biddle—as, unfortunately, she had—her insides thrummed.

Maybe her sister had a point. Maybe she liked her men…complicated.

"You are going to end up all alone with a closet full of fancy suits," Valerie had teased when Jamie passed her dateless twenty-fifth birthday.

So within a year Jamie had rekindled the thing with Donald, her tame college boyfriend. Stable, convenient and deadly dull, Donald was still living in Kansas City, practicing routine law. Living in Tulsa while Donald lived in KC hadn't bothered her, because their relationship had always been long-distance. That should have been her first clue. But within six months they were going through the motions of being an engaged couple, and Donald suddenly became not-so-convenient. He started insisting that Jamie give up her career now that they were ready to "settle down" in Kansas City. Jamie came to the conclusion that going it alone was better than living a life she'd hate with a man she felt lukewarm about.

Even though she'd been relieved when she broke it off, extracting herself from that long-standing relationship had caused Donald, her family and herself considerable anguish. The next guy, she decided, was going to have to be well worth risking that kind of entanglement. He was going to have to absolutely knock her socks off.

But who would have guessed that the guy who would knock her socks off would turn out to be a reclusive murder suspect? She looked at the face on the screen, and suddenly that face, which she had seen in all kinds of poses, looked completely new to her. Studying old footage and photos of Nathan Biddle hadn't been the same as meeting him in person.

"Somebody out there to see you." Dave burst through the door, and Jamie jumped. He stood balancing a stack of older tapes and frowned at the handsome face on the screen. "He's a different kinda guy, isn't he?"

She hit the fast-forward button. "Who's out there?"

"You ain't gonna believe this. The DA."

"Trent Van Horn? Here?"

"Yep."

WHEN SHE SPOTTED Van Horn standing in the dimly lit reception area, Jamie's first thought was, *My, don't we look pretty tonight.* Apparently he was on his way to a "do," dressed in a formal tux, with a red cummerbund to boot. His patent-leather shoes mirrored the low after-hours lighting, his longish hair shone silver where it was slicked back from his temples, and his pungent aftershave permeated the air. No one else was about. Even the receptionist had taken off for the day. Good. Maybe she could get Mr. Van Horn to speak candidly for a change.

"Trent. How are you?" Jamie put out her hand first.

"I'm fine, Jamie." He gave her the standard handclasp. "I called and they told me you were still working at the station. I apologize for dropping by unannounced, but when I got your message, I figured you'd want a statement for the ten-o'clock broadcast."

Jamie didn't bother to respond to his self-serving apology. If Trent Van Horn wanted to stop by the station unannounced, he did it, no excuses needed. Jamie knew he wanted his face on the ten-o'clock news in the worst way. Shortly after taking this job in Tulsa, Jamie had figured out that Van Horn considered the media a handy extension of his campaign machine. *Opportunistic* didn't even come close to describing the man. But normally she would be the one summoned to Trent's door, like a serf before a landlord. So something deeper was at work tonight.

"What can I do for you?" Jamie wanted Van Horn to believe, always, that she was accommodating him.

"You were out at the Hart Ranch today?"

Uh-oh.

"Yeah. We went out there to shoot a teaser—from a distance—right after the body was found."

"And?"

Jamie weighed the situation. *Subpoena me if you*

want to know. "And nothing. Has the medical examiner told us the cause of death yet?"

Trent shook his head, apparently letting her evasion go.

"Can you give me a quick interview? Verify a few facts for me?" It would sure be helpful to make Van Horn her second source on this story.

Van Horn shrugged. "Of course. If it will help."

She stepped up to the reception desk and reached over the counter for the phone. She buzzed the editing bay. "Dave. Studio One's open, isn't it? Mr. Van Horn has kindly agreed to give us a sound bite for our ten-o'clock package."

It turned out to be a very disappointing piece of tape. Jamie had Dave shoot it as a stand-up, trying to create a feeling of immediacy, but the DA, as pompous and long-winded as ever, revealed absolutely nothing. When Van Horn got through talking *at* Jamie, she and Dave took the footage to the back and tried to make something interesting out of it.

"Another Trent Van Horn commercial." Jamie sighed.

"From what he says, I gather it's not his case, exactly," Dave observed.

"Not exactly. The body was found over in Osage County. But, of course, Van Horn is maintaining that Susie Biddle was moved there *after* she was killed here in Tulsa."

"Of course?"

"He wants to prosecute this on his turf, Dave. This is high-profile stuff. Susan Claremont Biddle was connected to half the big-oil-money families in northeastern Oklahoma."

"Oh. So does he have a suspect?"

"If he does, he's not saying, but my guess is it'll be the husband."

"Our big wild-looking dude, huh?"

Jamie nodded.

Dave whistled softly. "Heavy. At least we got that great footage of him out on the ranch today. You saving that for ten? Gonna weave it into this package or something?"

"No. We're not using it."

"Not—!" Dave's head jutted forward on his skinny neck. "Lady, that's some of the coolest footage I've ever shot. He looks like some kind of throwback brave, up on that horse with his eyes going all furious and misty and everything, and you aren't even gonna use it?"

"Look, Dave, if you wanna work at the pound, you gotta gas a few puppies. I know it's great footage. But I have my reasons for burying it."

"Man! I bust my rear night and day to make you look good, and that ain't easy, sister, keeping that hair out of the backlighting and keeping those chewed-up stubs off camera." He pointed at her ragged nails. "And this is the thanks I get—you're killing some of the greatest emotive footage I've shot since I started in this business. I zoomed right in on his eyes at just the right instant. Man!''

Jamie ignored Dave's rant while the images on the screen flickered on. Her eyes were seeing Van Horn, but it was Nathan Biddle's face that haunted her. Again she saw him in that moment of breathless silence after she told him about his wife. And Jamie, who could read a face as plainly as printed words on a page, knew what she had seen. For one instant his deep-set black eyes had blazed under the shadow of the cowboy hat as he fixed them on some point distant in time and space. Then tears pooled and were blinked back. She had noted the bitter set of his mouth. The painful swallow. It was great footage. The proverbial picture worth a thousand words. ''Nathan Hart Biddle,'' she whispered.

Dave sighed in resignation. ''So how come you think he did it?''

Jamie turned from the computer. If Dave's youthful naiveté hadn't been so clearly visible in the oblique lighting from the screen, she might have popped him one on the back of his dense head.

''That's just it, Dave. I *don't* think he did it.''

CHAPTER THREE

BRAD ALEXANDER waited with his headlights doused. Only after he saw his boss's black Ford Taurus swing around the corner of Frankfort and Third, did he ease his BMW out of the alley and into the Channel Six parking lot. He killed the Beemer's engine and punched in a number on his cell phone. "We need to talk. I'm in your parking lot… Trent just left?" he said as if he didn't know. "Oh. He gave you an interview? Great. I'll be right in."

Inside, the place was nearly dark, battened down for the nightshift. Peppy commercial music from a back room told him someone was working, feeding the beast, as they said in this business. "Ms. Evans?" he called out.

"Here." Her voice came from down a long dimly lit hallway. Someone was standing behind her. That skinny kid—the cameraman who seemed perennially glued to her side. He had shaggy hair and wore an earring, was probably a fag.

As Brad watched her silhouette walking toward him—tight straight skirt, mile-long legs—he noted again what a fine piece of woman Jamie Evans was. Too bad they weren't getting to know each other under better circumstances.

"I wouldn't normally come to the station," he started, "but I can't believe what I just heard. One of the detectives said the Osage County Sheriff spotted your Channel Six vehicle out on the Hart Ranch today."

"Shot a teaser," Jamie shrugged. "It's not illegal."

"It was stupid as hell, Ms. Evans." He leaned sarcastically on the *Ms.* as if it was an insult. "If I'm going to feed you tips that give you the advantage on this story, I expect you to show a little discretion."

"Discretion?"

"Biddle. If he spotted you, you alerted him."

"Alerted?"

"You know what I'm talking about." Brad's eyes narrowed on her. "You talked to him, didn't you? You realize you may have given Biddle time to hide important evidence. What did he say, what did he do, when you told him poor Susie's remains had been found?"

"What did he do?"

"Ms. Evans," he ground her name out through clenched teeth. "Echoing the question is an old lawyer's trick. Do you want to keep using me as a source on this story or not?"

As soon as he said it, Brad wished his mouth

had an "undo" button. He felt his nostrils flare as he fought to rein in his temper, reminding himself that *he* was the one who needed Jamie Evans.

"Do you *want* me to keep using you?" When it came to the DA's office, sometimes Jamie wondered who was using whom. She wasn't about to admit she'd talked to Biddle. Alexander's eyes had flashed with such fury just now that she thought he might actually strike her.

"Thanks to your little teaser, *Ms.* Evans, we'll have to hustle to get a search warrant out there, maybe even tonight."

"A search warrant?" Jamie's pulse shifted into high gear. "For what?"

"I'm not inclined to tell you." Brad's voice was petulant.

"Now, Brad." She tried for a conciliatory tone. Even if Brad Alexander did grate on her nerves, big time, how often did a neophyte reporter connect with a powerful source like this? The First Assistant District Attorney. She didn't exactly understand why he was coming to her, and she even wondered if Brad the Brat, as she and Dave liked to call him behind his back, had the hots for her or something. She scrubbed that very revolting thought. But Brad definitely had some kind of hidden agenda. "Look. I'm sorry I went out there. But the M.E. was my official source on that one, and you should have told me Biddle was a suspect. Now, what are we looking for?''

"Did you get video of Biddle?''

"Nothing useful,'' Jamie said. She knew what was coming next. Segments of news video had ended up in courtrooms before. "What are we looking for?'' she pressed.

"Probable cause.''

Employing that *we* bit worked every time. Brad seemed suddenly cooperative now that Jamie had something he wanted.

He went on, "The cops have circumstantial evidence, motive—''

"Motive?''

"Yes. The Biddle marriage was strained. If they split up, she would have taken him for half of everything—the ranch, the mansion, the oil royalties.''

Jamie frowned. Nothing in her investigation had indicated marital problems. How had the police— and Brad—gotten this kind of information? She made a mental note to find out.

Brad was still talking, checking his list off on his fingers, "We have opportunity, witnesses, everything but modus operandi, which, in a crime of passion, wouldn't apply. Now we need some physical clues. A knife, specifically. The autopsy showed a significant marring, a scrape on the clavicle, which would indicate a slashing or hacking wound.''

Jamie could feel Dave cringing beside her, but she pressed on while Alexander was in the mood to talk. ''A cut across the collarbone. Was *that* the cause of death?''

''Probably not. The M.E. thinks it was a fall— she had a broken neck. But the wound would have been significant, too, possibly from a large hunting knife.''

Dave made a shocked little noise, then said, ''There would have been a lot of blood. You know, bloody residue wherever…the, uh, injury took place…'' His voice trailed off.

''So then, out at the ranch,'' Jamie asked, ''they're probably going to do that test you told me about once? The one where the black light turns old bloodstains blue? Whaddaya call it?''

Suddenly Brad looked worried, and a warning blip crossed Jamie's radar. ''Yes. Luminol,'' he said absently. ''They'll spray the walls, the furniture, maybe even rip up the carpet.''

Jamie waited for him to go on, but he didn't, so she scrambled for more questions, anything to keep him talking. ''So they'll test those surfaces for blood residue, for DNA evidence?''

''Yes, DNA,'' Alexander said, clearly distracted now.

''What about the Biddle mansion here in

Tulsa?'' Jamie pumped him. "Are the cops going to spray there, too?"

"Of course."

Jamie's source was drying up right before her eyes. He checked his watch. She quickly said, "And what about that neighbor who overheard them having a loud argument the night Susan Biddle disappeared?"

Brad seemed surprised that she knew about that, and the question brought him back into focus. "Old Mrs. Petree has passed on unfortunately."

"But you guys still have her deposition?"

"Yes."

"Now what?" Jamie pressed.

"Van Horn will get the Osage County Sheriff to go out and search the Hart Ranch immediately. We can get a search warrant for the Tulsa home from a judge here first thing tomorrow." Brad's eyebrows shot up and he checked his watch again. "Listen. I've got to go."

"Wait," Jamie said as he backed up. "Will they search the whole ranch? And when will they do this search?"

"Tonight, if possible."

"You'll tell me when they go?"

"Yeah, sure. Yes," he repeated more emphatically, then stopped in his tracks, seeming suddenly intent on that idea. "In fact, I'll page you. You're thinking of covering it?"

"Absolutely." Jamie shot Dave a look, and Dave arched an eyebrow as he tugged on his earring. "Maybe we can even get the chopper," he muttered.

As Brad watched their exchange, he felt less tense, more in control. The reporter and her skinny shadow would be on that ranch like stink on shit, and a little media ruckus would prove a very useful distraction. He'd make sure Van Horn let him organize the search warrants so he could stall to allow himself enough time. Now if only the tall grasses were very dry and the winds were blowing just right...

THE *CUT-CUT-CUT* of the Skyranger Six chopper blades always made Jamie jumpy. Somehow, the monotonous beating seemed to intensify her motion sickness. The tiny helicopter rocked in the wind like an empty soda can on a string. She glanced back at Dave, all cozy in the rear seat, surrounded by his equipment, chewing a wad of gum, happy as a clam. The pilot was grinning from behind his aviator sunglasses. Jamie hated them both because they never got airsick.

"Not far!" the pilot hollered over the noise. "Sorry for the bumpy ride!" He pointed. "Over there's the tallgrass prairie. Largest expanse of native tall grass remaining on this continent."

Jamie and Dave exchanged smirks. They had

nicknamed this pilot Encyclopedia Jones because of his tendency to spout arcane facts.

The sun was just coming up at their backs, casting the rolling Osage Hills in a cool lavender light. To their right, the endless Tallgrass Prairie Preserve reflected the soft peachy hues of dawn. Rising clouds in the distance promised a thunderstorm later in the day. Despite her nausea, Jamie loved this part of her job—these rare moments when she got to see the natural world from the vantage point of the helicopter window. Pure magic.

"I didn't think old Phil was going to go for this, did you?" Dave bellowed from the back seat.

"Yeah. He's pretty stingy with this bird," the pilot agreed.

"I guess nothing else newsworthy is going on at dark-thirty," Jamie joked. It had been a late night, convincing Phil Hooks that the helicopter was the only way to get out to the Hart Ranch in time to catch the search and possible arrest of Nathan Hart Biddle.

Soon she recognized the river and the landscape of Hart Ranch ahead, then made out the barns and outbuildings—and the three sheriff's cruisers parked in an open triangle in front of the ranch house.

"They're here," she called over her shoulder to Dave. "Start shooting."

"I'm way ahead of you." He'd already begun.

The pilot angled the chopper to give the photographer an unobstructed view, and Jamie felt her stomach twist. She clutched her barf bag close. Then she saw something that distracted her. "Does that look like smoke?" She leaned toward the pilot and pointed.

In the distance a hazy column rose from the rolling hills, wavering in the dawn light. The pilot glanced once, didn't seem to see. Dave was filming the cruisers and ranch house, now directly below them. Jamie looked down. No activity was visible. Jamie wondered if they'd pulled Nathan Biddle out of bed, wondered if he'd figured out the awful truth by now.

She glanced toward the sunrise again, and this time she was certain she saw smoke. "Go that way!" she commanded over the noise.

"Boss didn't authorize a bunch of running around, lady. This thing eats fuel, you know."

"That could be a fire!"

"So? Out here on the tallgrass prairie they set fires all the time to burn off that pesky Japanese grass."

"A controlled burn? With the wind gusting like this? Besides, it's over by part of the Hart Ranch. Isn't that the plateau where we filmed yesterday?" She directed this question to Dave, but didn't wait for the answer. "That's near that old cabin. It can't be more than a couple of miles. Fly over and check it out. I'll take responsibility for the fuel.''

The pilot made a sour face and practically turned the chopper on its side, making Jamic's sweet roll and coffee lurch up dangerously. He flew at full speed toward the smoke on the horizon. Jamie pointed as they passed over the roof of the old cabin, barely visible through a thicket of dry-leafed blackjacks. As they got closer to the column— large and definitely smoke—the fire itself became visible. Flames made eerie Z's on the gray hill-sides, and the pilot immediately changed his tune.

''That's a big one, all right,'' he said. ''We'd better not fly any closer.''

''Holy shit!'' Dave exclaimed while filming.

''That's no controlled burn.'' Jamie was already digging out her cell phone. ''I'm calling it in.''

She made a hasty call to alert the station first, then she punched 911, wondering if the cruisers on the ground a mile behind them would be called into the act. She told the dispatcher who she was, that she was looking at a massive grass fire, clearly out of control, headed directly for the Hart Ranch complex. The dispatcher took careful coordinates of their location, with the pilot shouting out land-marks over the chopper noise.

Just as she'd figured, Jamie was ordered to stay on the line while the dispatcher contacted units from the nearby town of Pawhuska. She covered the mouthpiece and shot a look of disgust back at Dave. "I have to hold." She studied the fire. "It's definitely moving southwest," she muttered toward the window.

Suddenly she turned her head and shouted to the pilot, "Head back to the ranch! We've got to warn them."

The pilot did another sickening turn and flew full throttle toward the ranch house. They landed near the cruisers in a cyclone of dust, and immediately the sheriff came marching out of the ranch house, looking angry, waving them away.

Jamie jumped from the door while the blades were still rotating. With the cell phone pressed to her ear, she held up her free hand in placation. "Prairie fire!" she yelled. "Out of control! A mile or two northeast!"

The big man cupped his hands and shouted, "Did you call it in?" as they ran toward each other.

"Yes!" Jamie's throat was so dry she no longer felt any nausea. "Pawhuska's sending units. I'm on hold with the 911 dispatcher."

"I'll take over!" the sheriff said. "Give it to me!"

Jamie handed him the phone.

"You with Channel Six?" he asked as he held the phone to his ear, waiting.

"Yes." Jamie paused to catch her breath as

Dave and the pilot jumped out and rushed toward them. Dave filmed as they stood in a cluster, telling the sheriff as much as they could about the fire. "We may need you to go back up and call in the exact parameters of the fire," the sheriff said. The pilot nodded.

Nathan Biddle emerged from the ranch house with the two deputies on either side of him. At the sight of him, Jamie's pulse—already racing—quickened even more. The sheriff called out the situation before they'd gotten halfway across the yard. Biddle stopped and turned, hollered something urgent to one of the deputies. An argument ensued. Jamie could only catch the words *high-strung thoroughbred* over the chopper's noise.

Biddle finally made a cutting motion with his arm, then turned and ran in the direction of the barns. The deputies trotted over to the group. One faced the sheriff and said, "The man's got a high-dollar stud horse he wants to save and six brood mares. He says he can swim them all across the river."

"Wouldn't take no for an answer," the other deputy put in.

"Nathan ain't going nowhere," the sheriff said dryly. "Let him move his horses. We got bigger problems now, anyways, boys. The Tulsa DA can waste his own time trying to find some old hunting knife that ain't here."

Jamie wanted to ply the sheriff with questions, but he was shouting, "Yeah, Sheriff Bates here," into the cell phone.

"Okay," he said next. Then, "I've got the Channel Six Skyranger helicopter out here. They volunteered to go up and provide aerial support. Pawhuska will take fire-ground command. Until we know more, go ahead and have Blackpool's units go east on Highway Twenty." He stopped and spoke to the pilot. "You can get close enough to provide air guidance, can't you?"

The pilot nodded, and Jamie said, "I'm going back up with you. We'll do a phoner. Dave can feed back video."

A deputy passed a cell phone to the sheriff, and Jamie took hers back. She and Dave followed the pilot to the chopper. As they lifted off, Jamie looked down toward the barns. She saw Nathan Biddle, now wearing a tan cowboy hat and a dark leather jacket, mount his paint while he held three other horses on long leads. She watched him galloping toward the river for as long as she could before they all disappeared under the dense canopy of blackjacks.

In the wind and shifting smoke, it was all the trio in the helicopter could do to keep their bearings and identify roads and landmarks. They made a wide circle, spotted two other dwellings in the immediate path of the fire, and called in the locations of these. By the time they circled back, fire-fighters from six towns had arrived with twenty units to battle the blaze. The wildfire was suddenly the day's big media event.

"The fire is eating up everything in sight," Jamie reported, while Dave fed digital pictures back to the station.

Jamie was so caught up in the moment that she completely forgot about Biddle until she spotted him again, this time riding at a hard gallop toward the old cabin up on the plateau. The horse he rode now was black, huge and powerful. Its pounding hooves created an enormous ribbon of dust in the dry morning air. The fire, snaking around the base of a hill, was making its way up to the plateau like a hot orange army on the march.

"Where's he going?" she shouted back to Dave as she poked her finger at the glass, indicating Nathan passing below them.

Dave leaned forward. "To that cabin obviously." He picked up his camera and twisted to get a good clean shot of the horse and rider.

"Turn around and land on that plateau by the cabin!" Jamie ordered the pilot.

"Ms. Evans, that fire is getting too close for comfort now—"

"Exactly! He wouldn't be taking such a risk without a reason. Now land this thing!"

They circled and touched down just as Nathan

Biddle threw himself from the saddle and raced full speed toward the cabin. Only then did Jamie see the old motorcycle parked under the sloping shed roof supported by two log poles. Someone was in there.

She jumped from the chopper and ran, feeling rather than seeing Dave on her heels. Up close, the cabin looked like something out of a movie about pioneers: chinked-log construction, a fat stone chimney that seemed larger than the little box of the cabin itself, drying gourds hanging on exterior walls.

"Wow!" Dave exclaimed as he filmed.

As they burst through the open door, Nathan Biddle, his jeans soaked to the skin, was standing with his back to them next to an enormous shirtless man with a long black ponytail, who was lifting a large wood-framed drawing off the rough-hewn wall. It was a yellowed charcoal sketch of a swan in profile, done in bold black lines.

Jamie sucked in her breath when she saw what Biddle held. An Osage war shield! The unmistakable white markings on stretched buckskin, the five eagle feathers hanging at the bottom, two others strategically placed at the top. Surely it was some kind of copy. No authentic Osage shield existed outside the protection of a museum these days.

Biddle turned from his task and squinted at her in horror. "What the hell are you doing here?"

"We landed outside," she explained as if anyone within a mile couldn't hear a helicopter landing. "That fire's closer than you think and the road's covered in smoke. I've got the chopper outside. We'll lift you both out. Let's go!"

The big man beside Biddle said, "I will get the bound volumes. You get grandfather's Peyote fan and crucifix." Biddle nodded and swung around with the shield, headed for a battered old dresser. The other man crossed to some crude bookshelves in the corner, seeming to dominate the room as he moved. "Do not film these objects," he quietly commanded Dave as he passed near him.

Dave obediently lowered the camera. "Okeydoke," he muttered under his breath, and gave Jamie a wild-eyed look as he angled the viewfinder upward and the tape heads continued to turn.

All over the cabin were other Osage artifacts. Blankets, beaded work, paintings. And shelves and shelves of books, stacks and stacks of papers, piled on a rickety drawing board shoved under the one grimy window. Surely they weren't trying to save all this stuff.

"Mr. Biddle, I don't know what you're trying to do here—" she held out her hands imploringly as she stepped toward Nathan "—but we don't have much time." In fact, the smoke seemed to be getting thicker in the air that gusted into the open doorway.

Biddle stopped what he was doing, turned and stared out the door. "Robert," he called to the big man who was unplugging a laptop computer, "you must go now. I'll stay behind and gather his papers."

"No," Robert answered as he pulled several oversize leather-bound books off the shelves. "I'll stay. You go. I have the Indian."

"And how much gas have you got in that thing?" Biddle argued. When Robert didn't answer, he said, "That's what I thought. And what about Bear?"

Jamie realized that the Indian must be the ancient-looking motorcycle parked out front, but who was Bear? Her question was answered when a large butterscotch-colored dog lumbered in from the back porch area. He looked part chow chow or mastiff. He'd been drawn by the sound of his name, she supposed. "You don't understand," she pleaded. "This fire is *huge*. Take the dog if you want to, but *please*, we must go. Now."

"Not until we get our grandfather's things," Biddle informed her as he kept working steadily.

"You're risking your life—and *ours*—for some dusty old books and a fake Osage shield."

Robert never stopped in his efforts, but Nathan turned to her, and the look in his eyes could have frozen water. "*Nothing* in this cabin is fake," he said.

"I didn't mean..." Jamie faltered. "Just hurry. Please."

But when they got outside, the pilot had bad news. He climbed out of the chopper as Dave scrambled into the back seat. He eyed Robert and pulled Jamie aside. "That guy weighs three hundred pounds if he weighs an ounce," he told her, "and this chopper's only designed to lift three average-size adults, plus a little equipment—and *no* dogs."

"What are you saying?" Jamie asked, but she knew. Through the chopper's window, she saw Dave, staring straight ahead, protectively clutching the thirty-five-thousand-dollar camera issued to his care. Leaving the equipment—and the precious film—behind would only save them about twenty-five pounds, anyway.

"I can't take everybody, especially...oversize personnel." The pilot's aviators reflected the orange-tinted plumes of smoke beyond the ridge. "The big guy stays."

"The hell he does." The voice behind them was Nathan Biddle's.

Jamie hadn't noticed that he'd walked up. "Mr. Biddle, I—"

"My cousin goes, and so do all my grandfather's papers and effects. And so does the dog."

Jamie and the pilot turned their heads to look at the large man Biddle had called his cousin. He'd pulled on a grimy T-shirt and stood silently, with the volumes tucked under his meaty arms like rescued children. The large dog cowered against his thigh.

"This bird will only hold so much weight," the pilot insisted. "It's either you two or—"

"Then I'll stay," Jamie jumped in.

"We both will," Biddle turned to her, calm reassurance radiating from his dark eyes. "The horse can swim us across the river, if necessary."

"The boss won't like this. Me leaving his star reporter behind," the pilot argued.

"I won't let anything happen to Ms. Evans," Biddle replied.

"I'll drop these two and circle right back." The pilot, clearly frustrated, clearly frightened, looked up at the smoky sky. "Let's hope the wind doesn't shift, and the smoke doesn't get too dense, and my fuel doesn't run out."

Jamie placed a hand on the pilot's shoulder. "You'd better get going."

Biddle stepped over and grabbed the sleeve of Robert's T-shirt. "Get in," he said in answer to Robert's pained expression. Then he gave his cousin a shove. Once Robert was seated, Biddle bent forward, lifting the picture and the shield, setting them gently onto his cousin's lap. Then he lifted the old dog's hindquarters until he got him tucked safely between his cousin's large boots.

"Take care of Bear—and our grandfather's things."

Robert, who had been mute until this point, turned his face toward Nathan, and Jamie saw that his dark eyes brimmed with meaning. "No, my brother. Not his things. I will take care of our grandfather."

The pilot cranked up the rotors and as Jamie ran backward to get clear of the blades' blast, she stumbled. Biddle was right beside her and she felt his strong hand grip her arm. He practically lifted her off her feet as he circled a muscular arm around her waist and hauled her back. Not only did his touch feel powerful, it felt…stunning.

He lowered her to her feet and she turned away from his face, pretending to cough at the dust, afraid that her expression would betray how profoundly that moment of contact had affected her. As she turned to watch the chopper lift off, she saw Dave in the back window, with his camera against his face. Naturally, he had filmed the entire embarrassing encounter.

She started to say something smart to ease the tension, but when she turned, she saw Nathan Biddle's broad back and long legs striding away from her. He crossed through the smoky churned-up air and pulled the motorcycle backward out of its parking place. He started rolling it toward the narrow road that led down off the plateau.

"I thought you said it didn't have any gas," she said breathlessly as she trotted up beside him.

"It doesn't. Robert runs around on fumes half the time." He kept on rolling the machine at a good clip until they were out onto the road. "Don't worry. The stallion won't run out of gas."

Jamie was completely confused. "Aren't we gonna take the horse with us?" she asked.

"We'll come back for him." He mounted the motorcycle. "The cycle's noise would've spooked the stallion," he explained as he fired up the engine. "And he'll be testy enough, with both of us riding him out of here and smoke everywhere. Get on." He reached for her hand.

Jamie, suddenly wishing she'd worn a pantsuit that morning, gave him her hand and let him guide her onto the seat behind him. She fit her thighs around his hips, futilely tugging down on her slim short skirt. She gave up as he lurched away, realizing she had bigger things to worry about than modesty. Though he seemed awfully sure of himself, she was not sure she should trust this man with her life.

They roared down the road, veering off onto a path that careened steeply down to a deep creek. When they got to the bank, he said, "Okay," and put out his hand for hers again, assisting her off the bike.

Jamie was totally confused now, but her confusion turned to utter shock when he dismounted and shoved the bike into the creek.

"What the…!" she cried as the water gurgled over the submerged vehicle. Was she in the hands of a crazy man?

"When the fire gets here, these dry cedars and blackjacks will go up like kindling, and so will that old cabin." He grabbed her hand yet again and pulled her back up the path behind him. "That bike is a priceless antique, the progenitor of the modern Harley," he explained as they climbed. "Robert would never forgive me if I didn't save it."

"Save it!" she exclaimed. "You just ran it into the creek!"

"Better than letting it burn to a crisp. He can restore water damage." He stopped climbing and looked down at her. "What do you suggest? Loading it onto the horse?" He raised his eyes to the veil of smoke scuttling over the treetops. "The wind's shifting. Come on." He jerked her along behind him. "We're not out of the woods yet. And as much as I hate reporters, I still don't want to see you get charbroiled."

CHAPTER FOUR

BY THE TIME they got back up on the plateau, Nathan didn't need to point out the changed and dangerous direction of the wind. The forty-mile-an-hour gusts plastered Jamie's hair over her face and made the smoke swirl thickly through the trees, up over the low roof of the tiny cabin.

Nathan looked toward the peach-colored sky, toward the roar and rush and snap of the monster fire. "The cedar trees at the edge of the tall grass have caught," he said as he pulled Jamie into the cabin, "and cedars explode." Inside he started grabbing things—a blanket, water bottles, flashlight, a box of snack cakes—from the mélange around them. He moved with amazing speed, as if he had radar, homing in on exactly what he wanted.

"Can I help?" Jamie asked as he snatched a small backpack off the floor.

"Look for his cell phone," Nathan ordered as he stuffed the items into the bag.

The debris around her seemed to multiply as Jamie tossed aside clothes and papers, searching frantically. She cursed Robert for being such a slob. "I don't see it!"

"Never mind." He stepped into the kitchen area, yanked two dish towels off a rod and wet them under the faucet. "Tie this over your face." He handed her one and put the other on himself. She placed the towel, which smelled of rancid cooking grease, over her nose and mouth. He reached around behind her head and tied it roughly. Then he grabbed her hand again and tugged her out the door.

The smoke outside was thick enough now to make Jamie's eyes smart. Nathan dragged her toward the stallion, tethered to a low tree limb near the cabin. The horse, sensing danger, was prancing backward, whinnying and straining against the lead. Nathan kept repeating, "Whoa, boy," as he approached, then he soothed the animal with expert hands. When the stallion stood quietly, he hooked the backpack over the saddle horn and mounted, fluidly, still murmuring calm intonations.

"Okay." He looked down at Jamie. "Up you go." He extended a strong broad hand.

She stared at the hand, then into the dark eyes squinting at her above the towel.

"Up I go?" she echoed, and swallowed.

He gave her a questioning frown, then leaned an elbow forward on his muscled thigh, bringing his eyes directly into line with hers. "Your pilot is never going to make it back here in time, Ms. Evans. I know that this animal is scary, but he happens to be our escape vehicle.'' His uncannily accurate guess rattled her even more. The place where she stood at this moment was as close as Jamie had ever been to a horse. Her lifelong fear of the huge beasts stemmed from a frightening childhood incident at a rodeo. He eased his boot out of the stirrup.

''Now put your foot in there, grab here—'' he twisted to demonstrate with a palm braced on the saddle pommel ''—and give me your other hand.'' He spread his palm downward again. Whoa, boy,'' he murmured as the animal danced away from Jamie.

Jamie's throat, already dry, stuck closed with fright, while unconsciously she stepped away from the horse, not toward it. As she fought to breathe, she sucked the towel tight against her open mouth. Though Nathan seemed to understand her fear, his reaction was less than sympathetic. ''Look,'' he said in a low, almost threatening, voice. ''I've got control of him now, but don't make me get down and lift you up here. I can't guarantee what this stallion will do then. He's not a saddle horse. He's a stud. So do as I say. *Now.*''

Jamie blinked against the smoke and stepped forward. As soon as she did, the horse made a terrifying jerk and let out a frenzied whinny. Nathan used the reins and his voice to subdue the animal again. "Just step forward slowly," he urged Jamie.

She did so on wobbly legs.

"Now put your foot in the stirrup. Slowly."

The huge horse kept edging away. And it didn't help that Jamie's skirt was bunched practically to her waist. She struggled with all her might and tried not to think about the view Nathan Biddle might be getting—black bikinis beneath nude panty hose. As soon as she managed to get her foot in the stirrup, Nathan leaned down. With a hand hooked under her armpit, he hauled her up behind him. Somehow Jamie found herself straddling the saddle skirt. She wrapped her arms around him, clutching his waist.

"Keep your legs around his belly," Nathan told her. "Don't squeeze him back in the flanks. Kick him there, and he'll buck us off for sure."

That's reassuring, Jamie thought as she nervously scooted her feet forward on the horse's side.

"Just plant your feet on my calves," he said dryly.

"Okay," she squeaked.

"Here we go," he said.

With her eyes squeezed shut and her cheek mashed into the smooth cool leather jacket, she felt the horse lurch forward.

Jamie registered little about that jolting ride off the plateau. Except for the sound of Nathan's thudding heart and the feel of powerful muscle—both the animal's and the man's—she was aware of nothing.

She finally opened her eyes when she heard splashing water. She raised her head, coughing at the smoke, then felt cold water grazing her feet and found her voice. "Where are we?"

Nathan turned his head. "Hoshkahomi Creek. Unfortunately, not wide enough or deep enough to protect us. We'll have to make it to Middle Bird Creek."

Jamie looked around to get her bearings. Above the bare treetops, the morning sun was nothing but a weak spotlight now, shrouded in smoke.

They climbed the bank, hitting open ground, and the horse broke into a hard gallop. Jamie fumbled for a better hold, gripped Nathan's belt buckle and clung to his middle for dear life.

It seemed forever before they stopped. She looked around at the cedars and naked sycamores that dotted the landscape. Then she leaned around Nathan's wide back to look ahead of them. The horse stood on a rocky incline that veered toward the deep creek below. The trees on the opposite bank looked frighteningly far away. The rippling water looked too fast and deep for the horse, but as Nathan guided them down the embankment, she knew they were going to ride the stallion across.

"Where are we going?" Her voice was too loud,

too anxious, and she realized she was clutching his shirtfront.

"There's a narrow spot around the bend." His voice reverberated through his back, making a comforting vibration against her breasts.

But the contact was also disquieting, and she attempted to ease back, creating some space between their bodies. "What will we do when we get there?"

"Cross."

"Why don't we hear any fire sirens?"

Silence. He was leaning around the horse's neck to check the rocky ground ahead of them.

"Do you think the helicopter will look for us down here by the river?"

More silence.

"What will we do after we cross? Will we be safe then?"

"You sure ask a lot of questions."

"I'm a reporter."

The air was less smoky near the water, and she pulled the odious towel down and got a whiff of his hair, his neck, the leather jacket. He smelled like cut cedar and freshly laundered shirt—and something else purely virile and male. It was a smell that felt, at this precise moment, extremely safe. Jamie, who'd been so absorbed in her work, hadn't been this physically close to a man in quite a while. She closed her eyes, resisting the heady intoxicating *dangerous* urge to collapse against him. The circumstances made her feel this way, she reasoned, not the man. This man wasn't necessarily safe, she reminded herself. He might even be dangerous.

They came around a narrow meander in the river, and Nathan brought the horse to a stop on an alluvial wash. "This is the place," he said as he turned the resisting animal to the river's edge. He gave a gentle kick as he guided the stallion into the water. "Hold on tight," he ordered.

Like I'm not already, Jamie thought. She clutched him so tightly that the hind bow of the saddle cut into her midriff.

Bird Creek in October was unpleasantly cold. Jamie couldn't help but think of the damage to her expensive suede pumps and two-hundred-dollar silk suit. But when the horse skidded unevenly on the rocky bottom, she forgot about her ruined clothes. Nathan leaned with all his power to keep them steady. The cold water crept up and soon the horse was swimming.

When the water reached her thighs Jamie sucked in a shocked "Ahh!" and Nathan turned his head. His teeth flashed white in the first smile she'd seen from this man. "Better chilled than burned to a crisp." But even as he said it, he pressed the warm undersides of his muscular arms over her hands.

"Hang on," he encouraged. "We're almost there."

Nathan and the horse handled the current masterfully, but when they bounded onto the opposite shore, the stallion turned mutinous. He tossed his head and reared, churning his forelegs high in the air as Jamie held on and again squeezed her eyes shut, plastered herself to Nathan's back and pressed her cheek against his powerful shoulder.

"Are you okay?" Nathan asked, when he had the animal under control again.

Jamie nodded against his back. She imagined he could feel her trembling clear through the jacket.

They climbed the bank and she felt him twist the horse around. She opened her eyes to see fire snapping over the ridge in the distance.

"There goes Grandfather's cabin," Nathan commented sadly.

"I'm so sorry," Jamie whispered. She didn't even want to ask about the ranch buildings—or that grand old house. "Are your other horses here on this side of the river?" she hoped to distract him from his losses.

"Somewhere." His answer was flat. "We can stop here for a minute." She felt him kicking his boot free of the stirrup. "Down you go."

Their legs bumped while she fumbled for the stirrup. Once in, she swung her other leg over the horse quickly, determined to demonstrate that she was as intrepid as he was. But her muscles were taxed and already stiffening with chills, and when she hit the ground, her legs felt weaker than water. She would have landed squarely on her behind if he hadn't tightened his firm grip on her forearm.

"Easy," he said as he dismounted.

Jamie nodded and found her way to an outcropping of rock and lowered herself shakily. Nathan tied the horse to a low branch.

"I'm sorry your clothes got wet," he said as he walked over to her and set the backpack down. He dug out the bottled water, twisted the cap off and handed it to her.

She drank greedily while he unfolded the blanket. She noticed the stitching over the breast pocket of his brown leather jacket then. The Hart Ranch brand, a heart with a centered "H" connecting to the edges.

"Your first wildfire?" he said as he wrapped the blanket around her shoulders.

"I covered a civilized little grass fire alongside Turner Turnpike once," she said, shivering. "We were actually afraid they'd put it out before we got there! Nothing like th-this. Wonder where that helicopter is?" She studied the sooty sky.

"Getting refueled, I expect. Probably over at the Codding Cattle Research Airport. He couldn't get through the smoke now, anyway." He glanced at her worried face and added, "They'll have Chinook and Black Hawk choppers dropping water at the head of the fire. One of them may spot us.''

''Aren't you cold?''

He shrugged. ''I'll live.''

''Are you sure we're safe?'' Jamie chewed at a fingernail.

''I imagine the creek will stop it here,'' he said confidently. ''But I'd like to move downwind of the smoke as soon as you've rested.''

''Then let's go.'' Jamie tried to stand, but immediately sank weakly backward onto her palm.

''Whoa there.'' He grabbed her, settling her back with the same gentle tone he'd used on the horse. ''You don't look ready to get back up on old Sweetie Pie yet.''

''S-Sweetie Pie?'' Jamie suppressed a laugh.

''You don't think that's a good name for him?'' Nathan, who had hunched down on his heels beside her, looked back over his shoulder at the horse.

Sweetie Pie had one nervous eye aimed on them.

''Why is that horse so wild?'' Jamie asked.

Nathan turned back to her. ''He's a stallion—a stud horse. Nature of the beast. Saddle horses are usually mares or geldings.''

''Oh.'' Jamie blushed.

''I knew he'd be hard to handle, so I took him out of the barn after I had moved the others across the river. But then the wind shifted and I didn't have time to go back to the river for the paint or to the house to get my pickup. Had to ride Sweetie Pie up the ridge to Robert's. You're afraid of horses, aren't you.'' He tilted his head and studied her.

Jamie nodded, but her eyes were fixed on something in the water. "Only one thing scares me more,'' she said through clenched teeth.

He frowned. "What's that?''

"Snakes!'' she squeaked as she scrambled up onto the rock, pointing at a quarter-size black object that sluiced through the water toward them like a periscope. She found her footing and backed farther up the bank of rocks. He had already positioned himself between her and the snake. Jamie thought that was gallant, but the thing just kept coming. Then he reached down, picked up a huge rock and waited. When the large snake slithered out onto the bank, he lunged forward and bashed the creature's head with the stone. Jamie turned away and after a second started breathing again.

He turned to her. "This is shaping up to be a really pleasant day, all in all,'' he said mildly. It surprised her, that he could have a sense of humor about search warrants, wildfires and snakes.

"Mr. Biddle—''

"Since I've already saved your life twice today, you may call me by my given name.''

This flippancy was a side of him she hadn't expected, either. Perhaps it was just the euphoria after a crisis. She'd seen that reaction before. Or maybe he was covering the despair, the pain he must be feeling now.

"Okay, Nathan. Thank you for getting me out of the fire." She started to sit back down, glanced at the bloodied snake not ten feet away, thought better of it. "And for killing that thing. Do you think it was poisonous?"

"Yep. Water moccasin."

"How can you tell?"

"See the white cottonmouth?"

"Yes. Interesting." But Jamie felt repulsed. "Thank you, anyway."

"No problem. As long as we're in a grateful mood, thank you for not using that teaser."

Jamie's jaw dropped. "How did you—?"

"I own a TV," he said blandly, then amended, "Actually my detective checked it out."

"The detective you hired to help find your wife?"

His eyes clouded behind a dark defensiveness. He turned, took a couple of steps toward the creek. He stared out over the moving water for one moment before planting his hands on his belt and letting his head drop forward.

Jamie thought, *I shouldn't have said that,* as she studied his stance, his broad back. She knew he was thinking about his wife's body being found out in a river, on a muddy sandbar, hidden by brush.

"Are you afraid of me, afraid of being alone like this…out here?" he asked without raising his eyes from the ground.

"Afraid?" she stalled.

"They think I did it, you know. That's why the sheriff was sent to search my house this morning. They think I…I killed her. Do you believe that?"

"You haven't been accused—"

"But I will be. Do you believe I killed my wife?" He didn't turn around, but his posture was tense.

"I…no. Actually I don't." As she said the words, she realized she was speaking the truth. Something about this theory—a theory that Brad Alexander was already advancing—the idea that the Biddles had argued and then he had killed her in a rage, seemed impossible now that she'd met Nathan Biddle. He didn't act like a man who was ruled by his emotions or like a man who was hiding anything. And certainly not like a man who was afraid of anything.

Now he turned, studied her. His eyes were not cold, exactly, but there was a definite reserve in their depths. "Why not?"

"Because, Mr. Biddle—Nathan… I guess you could call it instinct or intuition. That's the strongest tool an investigative reporter has. And the hardest to come by. You see, in a strange way, I feel like I already know you. I've...I've been researching you and your wife's disappearance ever since I moved to Tulsa.''

''Yes, I know,'' he said simply.

The detective again, Jamie supposed. Doubts suddenly assailed her. Was she being naive? What made her so sure this man hadn't killed his wife? Maybe he was a manipulator, a good actor.

But Jamie wasn't easily manipulated or easily fooled. She trusted her own judgment too much for that. No one had to make up Jamie Evans's mind for her. No one had to tell her what was real. And she'd studied tapes of the Biddles before the wife had disappeared. She'd seen them twirling around the ballroom floor with other couples at the governor's inaugural like the prince and Sleeping Beauty. Most of all she'd seen the look in his eyes when he'd found out about his wife—and that was only yesterday, she reminded herself.

''I feel like I know you,'' she said again, ''because I've found out so much about you in the past two years, about your life, about your...your wife and her disappearance.''

He looked at her over his shoulder, his eyes suddenly sharp with interest. ''Exactly what do you think you know?''

He was putting her down, Jamie thought, but again she didn't blame him. ''I know that you met in college, hung out with the same kids, came from privileged backgrounds. I know that you became a successful oil-and-gas developer, even though your family is rich, even though you could have opted to do nothing but live off your royalties. That…'' Jamie hesitated. This was hard to say, but here was the real reason she didn't think this man had killed Susan Biddle. ''I know that you spent all kinds of money on fertility treatments, that after your wife disappeared you quit your job and dedicated yourself to finding her for a solid year, that you spent every dime you had, hounded the police, launched an independent public-awareness campaign.''

''Okay.'' He held up a palm. ''So you're a good reporter,'' he said and bent casually to pluck up a pebble at his feet. ''But you had to have somebody feeding you information. You got out here before any of the other media, before the local sheriff, even before I myself was informed.''

Jamie felt a chill at his tone. He was being too calm. And she sensed he was digging for something important. What did he know about her source? She pulled the blanket tighter around her shoulders. ''Your detective again?''

''No, just a plain old guess.''

''A reporter can't talk about her sources.''

He studied the pebble for a moment before flinging it in the water. Then he checked the sky. ''We'd better head downstream.'' He walked over to the horse, talked soothingly to the tense stallion, then led the animal back to Jamie. She gulped another swig of water, then offered the bottle to Nathan. He took it and drank, then dropped it in the backpack and hoisted himself up in the saddle. "You know the drill," he said, and extended his hand to her.

Jamie stepped up to the horse, determined to do better this time, and this time it did seem easier—for all three of them—to get her aboard. Riding seemed a bit easier, too. They trailed along the creek at a trot for some minutes before Jamie got up the nerve to continue the conversation. She looked back at the roiling black smoke rising from the higher ground above them.

"That cabin. You called it your grandfather's?"

"Great-grandfather's, actually. The original old Osage. He built it in the 1890s, and even after the oil money came along in the twenties, when all the other Osages were throwing up fancy houses and driving brand-new cars he continued to live up there. Simply, in the old way. He was my father's grandfather. My grandfather Biddle married a chief's daughter, Ruby Hart."

"So Chief Black Wing was your great-grandfather?"

He turned his head, seeming surprised that she had produced the name. His eyes formed deep-set slits. "Anything you *don't* know about me?"

Jamie ignored the sarcasm in his voice. "Your cousin. Did he actually live in the cabin?"

"Yes."

Jamie waited, but he didn't offer more.

"Robert—that's his name, right? What does Robert do?"

"He helps me with the horses some, but mostly he fiddles with old pieces of paper—my great-grandfather's poems, transcriptions of oral Osage stories. Robert is—*was*—trying to save that stuff."

Jamie thought of the computer, the laptop Robert had gripped for dear life. "My God," she said. "You're telling me historical documents might have been burned up in that old cabin."

"Yes. Except the stuff we stuck on your chopper a while ago."

Mentioning the helicopter made her worry again. "How will they ever find us out here? The canopy of the trees—"

"We'll be out in the open soon, and we have the horse," Nathan continued calmly. "We can ride him all the way to Pawhuska if we have to."

The idea of riding ten miles on a testy stallion was not particularly reassuring to Jamie, especially in wet clothes with a backside that was already feeling sore. "You're sure we can find our way around the fire?" Jamie protested.

"As long as we stay on this side of Bird Creek, I think we'll be okay," he replied.

And then, as if nature were adding insult to injury, thunder rumbled in the distance. "Is that thunder?" Jamie asked unnecessarily, unable to contain her anxiety.

"Is that an investigative question?"

Jamie rolled her eyes. This guy was a riot. "I meant, are we heading into a storm?"

"I certainly hope so."

"You hope so? You want to ride this crazy horse all the way to Pawhuska in a thunderstorm?"

"Well, I'd sure hate to get all wet." Again the sarcasm—they were already soaked to the skin. "But then, I keep thinking about those poor firefighters—"

"You know I'm not talking about getting wet. This—" she lowered her voice to a hissing whisper for the next word "—*beast* will go crazy in a thunderstorm, won't he?"

She couldn't see his face, only the back of his longish black hair grazing his massive shoulders, and the edge of one jaw as he tilted his head down. Something about the line of that jaw told her he was grinning. "We'll be all right."

A flash of light paled the peach-colored smoky air. Lightning! Another long rumble followed, closer than the one before. Jamie didn't think her nerves could handle one more assault. "What if we get hit by lightning?" she hollered above the rising wind. She'd given up on keeping the blanket over her head. She'd given up on trying to keep warm or ever feeling her feet again, but she didn't want to fry from a lightning bolt out in the middle of the tallgrass prairie.

"Shouldn't we take shelter?" she insisted when he didn't answer immediately.

"Maybe. Let's see how the sky develops." He kept the horse trotting steadily forward.

The creek meandered beside smaller trees now, and before long the vegetation thinned to ground level. The long grasses out ahead of them whipped like waves on an endless sea. When the first fat raindrops fell out of the darkening sky, Jamie felt as if nature were spitting on her. First one, then several smacked her head, pelting her like buck-shot.

"All *right*," Nathan said approvingly. "This should help put out the fire." She watched his tan cowboy hat turn chocolate-dotted where the drops struck. Lightning, closer now, streaked over the sky and the prairie ahead. Jamie couldn't see so much as a tree or even a sizable rock in the swirling sea of grass.

Abruptly Nathan turned the horse and broke into a faster trot, heading back toward the woods.

"Now what?" she yelled above the rising wind.

"I'm afraid you're right about the lightning. We're going to have to retreat to lower ground, back down toward the creek bottom."

When they got to Bird Creek, he turned off into a rocky tree-sheltered cove. He levered her off the horse again, then eased himself down with athletic grace. He glanced at her worried face. ''Your guy wouldn't fly that bird into a thunderstorm, anyway, would he?''

Jamie, too uncomfortable to argue with this logic, mumbled, ''I guess not.''

''If anything,'' he said calmly, ''let's hope it's a deluge.''

Suddenly, as if he'd commanded it, the sky seemed to open up, and rain poured down in thick, shifting gray sheets, bulleting the creek, the rocks, the parched soil.

Now what? Jamie thought. In her wildest dreams she'd never imagined herself sitting out a thunderstorm on some cozy little rock in the middle of nowhere, having a nice conversation with a murder suspect.

CHAPTER FIVE

THAT WAS EXACTLY what they did. "Find a comfortable spot," he ordered, then led the skittish horse away. Jamie found a large low boulder and sat on it, hugging her knees and pulling the blanket around herself. But even with the blanket, she started to shiver.

Nathan tied the horse to a tree limb, then unhooked the backpack and joined her.

He removed his jacket and sat down, scooting close as he pulled the warm leather up over their heads, making a small tent. "Here," he said, and suddenly one strong arm pulled Jamie to his side. "Much as I hate 'em, I wouldn't want to see a reporter freeze to death."

Jamie's shivering immediately subsided. His side felt amazingly warm and his jacket smelled like a delicious expensive aftershave. If the circumstances had been any different, she would definitely have been enjoying herself. "Thanks," she mumbled.

"Don't mention it." He looked out at the pouring rain. "There's nothing we can do now but wait.

Unless you want to get up on Sweetie Pie over there while he's acting like that.'' The horse was nickering and flinching as raindrops pocked his rump like BB's, and every time thunder boomed, he whinnied again and reared in protest.

"Hold this up,'' Nathan said, and gave her the collar of the jacket. Then he dug the snack bars out of the pack. "Hungry?''

Jamie shook her head. She felt too enervated to eat.

"Better eat something,'' he explained as if he'd read her mind. "The pumping adrenaline empties the stomach, uses up your sugar stores. If you're gonna have the energy to get back up on Sweetie Pie…'' He waggled the cereal bar.

She took it. He tried to resume holding her side of the jacket up, but she said, "I've got it,'' and held the lapel out. It felt weird enough being pressed to him like this. She didn't want to feel the weight of his arm across her shoulders, as well.

He'd wolfed down his snack before she'd even managed to unwrap hers, using her free hand and her teeth. While she chewed, her mind turned to the topic of the cabin, because even though it was distressing, it was a relatively safe topic compared to the other things they might talk about. And her curiosity—barely under control in normal circumstances—had been absolutely strumming ever since they'd loaded those artifacts on the helicopter.

She swallowed the dry granola. "Was that war shield you took from the cabin really an Osage shield?"

He had picked up another stone, studying it. "Yes."

"Wow." Jamie took another bite of the granola bar and kept her eyes on him, hoping he'd say more. But he simply continued to study the rock. And she studied *him.* His features were strong and classic, his skin tan and smooth, and his eyes, dark and deep-set, retained an eerie calmness, a reserve, even when his words were sarcastic or teasing. His profile mirrored a strength that she suspected had been passed down to him with his genetic code.

"So. Tell me more about Black Wing," she prompted, hoping he would open up.

"Why? You've researched all this, haven't you?"

She had. "But if Black Wing was your father's grandfather, why did you and Robert refer to your grandfather's things?"

"With Native Americans any ancestor is simply called grandfather, but Chief Black Wing was actually my Grandma Ruby Hart's father, which would make him my great-grandfather." Nathan looked down at her, and for a moment those guarded eyes flickered with intensity. "You know anything about the Osages?"

Jamie shook her head. Actually she did have some layman's knowledge, but she knew that the more you feigned ignorance, the more information people volunteered.

"Hart was my family's white name, the one Black Wing adopted after the Daw's Commission, after they got their head rights."

"Oh? What was Black Wing's first name?"

There was a blank pause, as if he really didn't want to say, then he answered quietly, "Nathan."

"So you were named after him?"

"Yes. Robert claims Ruby Hart—my grandmother—insisted on it. Anyway, Ruby Hart married old man Biddle, my grandfather, a white man. They had my father, Jack. So all my Indian blood comes through my father, and the Osages don't really cotton to that. They followed the bloodlines of the mother."

"I think I read that somewhere." Jamie was fascinated, but didn't want to get him sidetracked too far into a lecture about Osage ways. She wanted to know about *him.* "So, what percentage Osage does that make you?"

He stared out at the falling rain, biting his lip as if weighing his answer, and she wondered if she'd said something wrong. Then she wanted to smite her forehead. "I'm sorry," she said. "I just remembered that when I was interviewing someone at a stomp dance in Ponca City, he told me that's an offensive question to some people.''

He glanced at her and his expression softened. She supposed—hoped—he could see the sincere regret on her face.

"It's natural to ask, but I've always hated the sound of that question. Not just because of the obvious connection between how much Indian you are and the distribution of head rights.'' He looked out over the rising creek again. "Although when bloodlines got tied to oil money, that's when the real trouble started for the Osages.''

"The reign of terror and all that.''

He sighed and threw the rock far out over the river. Then he turned to her. "Some folks will whip out their BIA card and tell you that percentage of blood is a matter of pride in their heritage, but I think talking about blood quantity is kind of insidious. As if we were pedigree stock or something.''

Jamie did understand. Completely. The idea of quantifying blood, by fourths, eighths, sixteenths, down to the tiniest drop, was abhorrent, really. Racist. But at some point the Indians had been forced to buy into it in order to protect what was theirs. She voiced her next thought out loud. "But I don't know if this new mixed-blood Native American wording is any better.''

Nathan smiled, admiration shining in his dark eyes. "Robert has a saying—it's what's in your heart, not the stuff that pumps through it, that makes you an Indian. You're lucky Robert isn't here. He'd have turned his back on you for asking me how much Osage I am."

"But *you* won't, I hope." It seemed as though they were reaching some kind of amity as they huddled under this jacket. Others in her profession had warned that he was a tough interview and he was. But ironically he was also an easy man to talk with.

"I'm not some self-righteous Indian." He released a huge sigh. "So, since you asked, legally I'm one-fourth Osage. When Ruby Hart, Black Wing's daughter, married my grandfather William Biddle, the Biddle ranch and the Hart's Osage lands were combined. I'm on the rolls, I inherited head rights, but you know all about that, I expect."

"I know you're the sole heir to this huge ranch."

"Yes. My dad had a brother, but he died in World War Two when he was only twenty. Actually Robert could lay claim to part of the ranch, but he refuses. Robert's a little on the eccentric side—"

"So I gathered."

"His grandmother was Ruby Hart's sister. The old chief didn't get any sons."

"I see," Jamie said, but she was beginning to think she needed a chart.

"Robert can live here as long as he likes. I think of the ranch as a retreat, and he does, too. On that score, our attitudes are the same. The ranch is our refuge and will remain so."

She believed that. He seemed so calm, so peaceful whenever he spoke of the ranch.

"Robert gets his head-right checks and that gives him the freedom to do what he really loves."

"Writing down the Osage oral history?"

"Right. And the poems. Mostly he's concerned with the poems. Black Wing used to recite the poetry out loud. Robert's mom was a teacher, and the old chief allowed her to tape him."

Jamie looked across the river, raised her eyes to the sandstone plateau where the cabin had stood. She suddenly understood the stubbornness of the two men when she'd tried to get them into the helicopter. "Were the tapes in the cabin?"

"The originals very well could have been. I'm not sure how much Robert saved. But of course, he's made copies. Probably has them deposited in the Western History collection at the University of Oklahoma." He glanced at her. His eyes were so dark, so deep that she felt a strange thrill every time he did so.

"That charcoal drawing?" she kept the conversation going. "The swan?"

"A family treasure."

Jamie noticed he didn't say "heirloom."

"It looked very old."

"It is. They say someone drew it for Black Wing—after his heart was broken, during the days after the Osages were moved from the place of the many swans."

"The place of the many swans?" Jamie's reporter's ears pricked up at the magic in those words.

"The Osages..." Nathan gave her a crooked little grin, "By the way, Robert always makes a point of calling them the *Wah-sha-she*—that's their original name. He's a purist, hates the way the French and then the English corrupted the tribal name into 'Osage.' Actually the old Osages called themselves Children of the Middle Waters. People think that's because they lived between the big rivers, but it isn't... Am I boring you?"

"Absolutely not!" Jamie realized she could probably listen to this man read the phone book. There was nothing boring about him. She found herself watching his mouth as he spoke. It was an amazing mouth. Strong, yet full, fluid, expressive.

"Anyway, to make a long story—a very long story that stretches back to the Ice Age, in fact—short, the Osages ultimately resided in an area around the Marais des Cygnes River."

"Mare de zeen?" Jamie echoed the name, loving the sound of it.

"That's French for the place of the many swans."

"The place of the many swans," Jamie repeated. "Why did they call it that?"

"I suppose swans nested there. It's the old Osage burying grounds in southwestern Missouri. When the white man moved the Osages to Oklahoma territory, forcing them to leave the ancient burial grounds, the swan became a symbol of all that was left behind, all that was lost."

"That picture must have meant a lot to your grandfather—I mean, your great-grandfather."

"They say it did. I remember looking up at that drawing when I was a very little boy. Back then I didn't appreciate all this. In fact, I hardly had any interest in my mother's family until…until I moved back out to the ranch. I guess, out here alone, I finally got quiet enough to appreciate the history. That picture, *The Swan,* has been in my family for generations."

"No wonder you didn't want it destroyed in the fire," Jamie said with a touch of awe. "Who drew it?"

"Robert thinks one of Black Wing's wives did. But there's a lot we don't know." He seemed sad for a moment. A heavy silence descended and the rain beat down on the jacket in a steady rhythm.

He broke his thoughtful mood, eyeing her. "Has this turned into an interview again, Ms. Evans?"

"Well, every conversation's an interview as far as I'm concerned." Jamie's answer was the truth. "I always love to hear people tell their stories."

"What I mean is, are you planning on using any of this in one of those 'packages' you're always winning awards for?"

Jamie colored. What did he know about her awards? Broadcast-news awards, certainly not well-known to the general public, were primarily a means of recognizing excellence within the industry. "Your private eye again?" She tried to appear casual, but when the investigative shoe was on the other foot, it pinched.

He nodded. "Let's see. An Edward R. Murrow. Two local Emmy awards. Best investigative-crime package of the year 2000."

"That about covers it," Jamie said, not wanting to talk about herself.

"Pretty good considering that you're only three years out of the gate. So am I the story that'll get you your next big award?"

"No!" Jamie protested. "I'm just doing my job to the best of my ability."

He made her sound like some kind of predator. She wasn't. She genuinely liked people and always tried to put a face on her stories. And she always managed to keep her ego firmly in check. Because in her business, media personalities rose and disappeared faster than shooting stars. Her first year out of journalism school, she had decided that if she climbed up the on-air ladder, it would be on the merits of her stories. She would have explained all that to him, but she wanted to keep the focus on his story. Lord knew when she would get the elusive Nathan Biddle to herself again. "Tell me about that shield you took out of the cabin. It's pretty old, right?"

"You *are* quick." His sarcasm, though gentle, was sufficient to chastise her.

"I'm sorry I called it fake. Like I said, I never imagined…" She faltered. "It was my understanding that such artifacts could no longer be found outside of museum collections."

"How would anyone know if they exist or not if they're hidden away in an old cabin by a slightly fanatical family historian? Robert swears the shield is real. Buffalo rawhide stretched on a willow frame, painted with blood-root juice."

"Wow," Jamie said, and Nathan smiled.

"But don't families usually donate that kind of stuff to collections?" she pressed.

"Not my family."

Jamie grew thoughtful, planning how to approach her next topic. The Harts had owned the combined land allotment, from which the head rights and the attendant royalty checks flowed.

From what Jamie was able to discover, Nathan had assumed his wife's disappearance was somehow linked to these massive family fortunes. He had been aggressive in his search for her. But how did he feel now that the search was over? She wondered how much he knew about the case being built against him.

"What do you think the sheriff was searching for this morning?"

"What do *you* think he was searching for?"

Jamie was not used to having the questions turned on her like this. "I have no idea," she said. The lie made her cheeks grow hot.

Nathan's dark eyes squinted at her, seeming to guess what she was thinking, then he turned his head toward the creek, and his expression became masked. "We both heard the sheriff mention my grandfather's hunting knife. But Robert has known it was missing for a long time."

Jamie's radar kicked in. The sheriff *hadn't* said it was Nathan's grandfather's knife. The sheriff had merely said it was an old hunting knife. "How long?"

"A couple of years. He noticed it was missing when he took inventory after he moved into the cabin."

"Who lived in the cabin before Robert?"

"No one. It had been unoccupied from the time of my great-grandfather's death." Nathan's sharp dark eyes assessed her again. ''Why do you ask these questions? Do you know something about the knife?''

''No. I always ask a lot of questions. It's my job.'' What made him think they were looking for his *grandfather's* knife? The thought snagged her mind like a sharp talon.

Nathan turned his face toward the ridge. ''Whatever they're looking for, it's gone now.''

Thinking about the fire still raging to the northeast gave Jamie a chill. ''You're assuming your entire ranch complex was destroyed?''

''The long barns are built of steel and the main house is as stout as a mountain—solid sandstone.'' He turned his head and stared off in that general direction. ''I can always restore it,'' he added quietly.

And with that simple comment, Jamie understood something more about the man's outlook. *Not easily defeated* was an understatement.

His straight white teeth flashed in a smile under the dim shelter of the jacket. ''This rain should have the fire dampened by now. Sorry about your pretty clothes.'' He gave a nod toward her soaked thighs, covered—or not so covered, actually—by shredded stockings.

''Uh, yeah,'' Jamie said senselessly. She, a woman who talked on her feet for a living, couldn't think of any intelligent reply. Because under his scrutiny, her heart was beating too fast and her throat was getting too tight. The sound of his deep voice so near, the feel of his warm breath brushing her temple…and his smell. It was all so incredibly…unreal. It was as if she'd been zapped into some alternative universe—*his* universe—and in this universe, an isolated ranch threatened by wildfire, everything was brighter, richer, more alive than anything she had ever experienced. She tried to ease her thigh away from his, but he only pressed closer, as if protecting her from the elements was an urge he couldn't suppress.

"We'll be okay," he said.

They stayed under the jacket until the storm passed. When the horse seemed approachable again, Nathan lowered the jacket, shaking the water from it. As soon as their shelter was gone, Jamie wondered what had happened to her while she'd been wrapped in that cocoon of warmth next to him. For something *had* happened during those few minutes of driving rain. Something almost chemical, a bond she couldn't define. As he stood, taking his warmth away with him, some part of her longed to be wrapped right back under the jacket beside him.

"Whoa, boy," he said as he started toward the skittish horse.

Jamie slowly stood, stretching her muscles and studying his back as he grappled with the animal.

She felt as if she was waking from some kind of altered state. She tried to shake it off. But she was too good a reporter to deny her feelings. Already her mind was recording memories of the way he felt, of his smell, of his—what was it? His *calm strength*. She had never experienced anything like it. *Attraction* was the only word she could think of, but that seemed too simplistic for the complex feelings that assailed her. She forced herself to walk forward, and the water squishing in her shoes brought her back to earth. "What now?" she said.

"The storm should have passed over the ranch by now and possibly put out the fire to the east, as well. I'd like to turn back and see what's left. We'll have to cross the creek again." He gave her a little smile over his shoulder as he stroked the horse's withers. "Don't worry. We're old hands at this. I won't let you drown."

But this crossing was vastly different than the one before. The creek was dangerously swollen now. Weeks without rain had baked the endless prairie to the consistency of concrete, and the creek had filled with runoff faster than a storm sewer.

Jamie's dressy silk skirt and business-cut jacket clung to her like a diver's wet suit as the horse dipped into the roiling waters.

Driftwood and loosened debris bumped their legs and the horse's side, making him even jumpier.

When they reached midstream, the horse lost his footing and panicked, fighting the current, stumbling sideways and rearing up.

Jamie felt herself tilt and slide on the slippery rump. She grabbed Nathan's jacket, and he grabbed for her arm, but they were both too late. Her thin wrist slipped from his grasp and the roaring creek sucked her down.

The water, crimson with Oklahoma red earth, instantly blinded her. Her feet could not find the bottom. Above the rush of the creek she could hear Nathan screaming her name, but all she could think about was air. Her head broke the surface and she gasped, only to go under again. When she came up again, she fought harder, slapping the water from her eyes. He was so far away! The current must have driven her downstream very rapidly.

Jamie was a competent swimmer, at least when she was doing civilized laps in the YMCA pool, but there was no fighting this torrent. She was being swept farther and farther away from Nathan, who called out to her in a diminishing voice: "Point your *fee-eet downstree-eem!*"

She tried to do as he said, but creekwater filled her mouth repeatedly as her head was submerged again and again.

Every time she came up, her blurred vision revealed Nathan on the horse thundering toward her through the brush on the creek bank.

When he reached her, he threw himself into the water and grabbed her by the scruff of the jacket. She felt herself being pulled back against the current, slammed against the hardness of his body and wrapped in the whiplike clasp of his arms.

"Breathe!" he commanded as he tilted her head clear of the rushing water.

She nodded, coughing and sputtering, panic seizing her because she couldn't seem to draw a free breath.

"Don't fight me!" he yelled, and swam to the bank with one arm. Jamie tried to help by kicking, but her legs felt numb.

He dragged her onto the muddy bank and Jamie felt herself, a dead weight, being flipped onto her back.

He wiped the mud from her face and said, "Come on, baby, breathe."

Jamie thought, *If only I could.*

He pressed his fingers to her neck, tilted his cheek over her mouth, then parted her blouse and pressed his ear to her chest. She felt him straighten her neck and head, pry her mouth open. A sweep of his rough fingers inside—and then he sealed his mouth over hers, wasting no time in starting CPR. All of this Jamie sensed as if apart from her own body, as if watching a drama where a woman lay dying and a man was doing his best to save her.

His breath felt hot and rich as it poured into her

throat, burning her lungs. She pushed him away with a forceful cough. He turned her head to the side and swept her hair back, letting her expel the brackish water.

Those first few breaths felt like fire, but he held her, rubbing her arms, her back, encouraging while she wheezed. "It's okay, baby. It's okay. You're okay."

Finally he lay her gently on her back and propped himself on one elbow, his worried face poised directly over hers, their harsh breaths mixing, the one warming the other.

Jamie nodded weakly, trying to tell him she was fine.

He seemed to understand. "You scared the hell out of me," he said, and flopped beside her, at last giving in to his own fatigue.

"Are you okay?" she managed.

His laugh was raspy, shaky. "I'm supposed to ask you that. You're the victim."

Jamie nodded, still gulping air.

They lay together like that for some moments, eyes closed, breathing in and out, their chests rising and falling in the desperate raking rhythm of the utterly spent.

When their breathing finally slowed somewhat, she looked at him and said, "You saved me from a wildfire and a drowning all in the same day."

He didn't open his eyes. "You forgot the snake."

"I'm not kidding. A startling chain of events has unfolded here today."

"Now I know you're okay. You sound like a reporter again."

"But that's really kinda...kinda weird, don't you think?"

"Yep." He sat up, inhaling and exhaling deeply. He planted one palm beside her shoulder and centered his face over hers. His cowboy hat was gone and his long hair drooped forward, muddy and tangled with twigs and dead leaves.

"I sure hope you're worth all this trouble." His face was solemn, but she saw a twinkle of humor in his dark eyes.

She smiled up into that face, which was becoming more familiar, more singular, by the moment. "You ain't seen trouble yet. Wait till I make you jump back in that creek to rescue my Sesto Meucci pumps." She wiggled her bare toes.

He shook his head and pushed himself up to a squat, resting back on his heels. "We'll have to forget your pumps, Ms. Evans—"

"Since you saved my life, you may call me Jamie." She gave him a teasing grin.

"Okay, Jamie. Time to get on the horse again."

She wondered what sort of picture they made as they rode up to the ranch house, where a sheriff's cruiser was parked out front. The cruiser, with the door wide open and the radio squawking loudly, looked like bad news. The ranch house, amazingly, showed no signs of fire damage.

"Everyone's been worried about you, Ms. Evans," the sheriff said as he strode toward them. "But I shoulda known Nathan would take care of everything." He gave their torn muddied clothes and her bare feet a skeptical once-over. "What the hell have y'all been up to out there?"

"Had a picnic, Jack. Took a swim." Nathan sank back in the saddle tiredly. "At least my place didn't burn." His voice held a note of gratitude as Jamie felt him slump back with relief.

"No, it sure didn't," the sheriff said as he came up beside the horse and grabbed the reins. "The wind turned the fire back off the ridge when the storm blew in. I expect your stock is still okay across Bird Creek, too. But all that'll have to wait."

Sheriff Bates fell silent. First he gave Jamie a regretful glance, then his puffy eyes focused on Nathan. "Nathan, I'm going to have to ask you to get down off that horse now." The heavyset gray-haired man stood with his legs braced wide apart.

Jamie panned her gaze from the sheriff on the ground up to the back of Nathan's head. He was staring straight ahead, looking at his ranch house. "Go ahead, Jack. Say whatever you have to say."

"Nathan, I hate like hell to have to do this." The sheriff looked up from under the rim of his battered hat and hitched his belt buckle up over his big potbelly. "But you gotta get down now, 'cause I'm gonna have to take you in."

Jamie kept her eyes on the back of Nathan's head. As far as she could tell, not one cell of his body moved.

When Jamie glanced down at the sheriff, all she could see was the top of his old cowboy hat, waggling slowly back and forth as the older guy shook his head.

"I'm sorry, Nathan," he said quietly from under the brim, "Looks like I gotta arrest you for the murder of your wife."

CHAPTER SIX

BRAD ALEXANDER parked on the shady side of the street. The ancient pin oaks and sweet gums in this older part of town towered pleasingly above, glowing with rich fall colors. He scanned the houses and yards, didn't see a soul. *Good.* Just as he'd thought, none of the residents were out and about among these gracious old homes at nine in the morning.

There would be quite a stir in the quaint neighborhood soon enough, however. He wondered how Nathan Biddle's tony neighbors would feel about a murderer in their midst.

He got out of the car and patted the thin bundle concealed in the vest pocket under his lapel. The weight of the thing pulled his jacket crooked, and the bulge, he realized, might be noticeable. He reached under his suit coat and fumbled until he got the object planted under his belt at the back.

He drew a deep steadying breath. What a fine day! He kicked a few colorful leaves aside as he hurried up the buckling old sidewalk, his mind alert, his plan perfect.

That plan, ridiculously simple, was to walk right up to the house, plant his little package in the grotto at the back and be waiting out front when the cops arrived.

The grounds of the Biddle mansion, densely landscaped and stretching more than a hundred yards to Woodward Creek, would provide plenty of cover once he entered the property. If he should happen to be spotted at any point along the way—by a construction worker, a yardman, someone of no consequence—he would have his reason for being there. Working on the Biddle case. His plan wasn't ideal, of course, but it was better than pitching the thing into the bottom of a lake. Why waste a perfectly incriminating piece of evidence?

Besides, he could march back to the grotto and be in and out and gone before anyone was any the wiser. He smiled.

The classic brick-and-limestone three-story, totally deserted for months, had a For Sale sign out front and one of those orange net construction fences unevenly tilting around the perimeter. Sun poured through the massive foyer windows. Two matching dormer windows on the third floor looked as blank as a dead man's eyes. As he climbed the hill, Brad could see yellow fall foliage reflected on the floor-to-ceiling corner windows of the formal living room. It was, he noted dispassionately, a truly lovely old home.

Brad had visited this place three times. Once, alone with Susie in the daytime. A thrilling event, forever burned in his memory. She had needed him then. And once, attending a massive formal fundraiser on the lawn for one of Nathan Biddle's endless pet charities. On that day, before everything had gone wrong, while he strolled the grounds with the other guests, he had noticed the little structure that would serve him so well now. A crumbling stone grotto, enclosing a small fountain in the back corner of the property. Concealed by heavy foliage. A charming footpath of flat stones led away from it, down toward the creek. The irony. Susie herself had come upon him and pointed out the loose square stone that slid out at the base of the grotto like a secret panel. While she was complaining about everything else in her marriage, she'd sighed and added that Nathan had been too busy to attend to the repair, and now she would have to take care of it herself. And finally there was that last time—that night.

Brad felt the familiar shortness of breath and quickly shunted all memory of Susie aside. He reminded himself—not for the first time—how convenient it was that his mind clicked on such small fortuities as that hiding place behind the stone. There must be a reason for such serendipity. Something to do with destiny. *His* destiny. Trent Van Horn himself had commented that Brad had a promising political career ahead of him. But political careers were not built upon foolish mistakes. So no more mistakes.

He found a gap in the orange fencing and slipped through. His alligator loafers tapped on the brick pavers with a purposeful rhythm as he marched up the hill toward the house, reminding himself that he had a good excuse for being here.

When he got to the side yard, he padded across a still-green patch of shade grass and cupped his hands to his temples as he peered into a tall beveled-glass window set deep in the stone wall. This, to create the illusion for any nosy onlookers that he was looking for something, instead of planting something.

"Lovely," he murmured in appreciation as he looked in on a stunning airy room that had been totally remodeled: fresh paint, stripped and stained oak flooring, new tiles. Nathan Biddle had gone all out to make the place marketable—or maybe he'd gone all out to wipe away his memories. But for Brad's purposes, the ripped-up carpets, the freshly sanded and varnished floors, the gleaming layers of new paint on the walls and woodwork, would serve another purpose, an incriminating one—and all too convenient.

He proceeded through a wrought-iron gate to the back of the house.

By turns shady and sunny, even in its neglected

state the backyard looked like a verdant setting off the pages of a home and garden magazine. Birdsong echoed in the high treetops, and a squirrel gave Brad a startled appraisal before scurrying off into the shrubbery.

Just a few more steps. He was grateful he hadn't encountered anyone so far. The idea of hiding the "murder weapon" on the perp's property was obvious, risky even, but all Brad wanted to do was make the pieces fit, keep the pressure on.

"Can I help you?"

Brad whirled at the sound of the voice and saw a man in white paint-splattered overalls, leaning out over the parapet of a small balcony. Only now did Brad notice the edges of scaffolding jutting around a wing of the house.

"Oh, hello," Brad responded smoothly. "I'm from the District Attorney's office. We're about to execute a search warrant here this morning, so I'm afraid you'll have to stop working."

"A search warrant? Oh. Because of the guy who owns the place, huh? I saw that on TV, heard how they found that poor lady—"

"Sorry," Brad interrupted. The last thing he wanted to do was commiserate about Susie. "I can't discuss the case." He stepped forward. "Have you been working here long?"

"A few weeks. The owner's been redoing the

whole place top to bottom for quite some time. Spending a lot of money. It's for sale, you know.''

''Yes, uh, I saw the sign out front. Matter of fact, my friend and his wife have been scouting this neighborhood. At one time they even expressed an interest in this very house.'' It was a total fabrication, but Brad thought the story had a nice disarming touch. ''Well, you'll have to leave, I'm afraid.''

''Sure.'' The guy shrugged.

When Brad flicked a glance up, he could see, even from this distance, that the painter was frowning down at him. ''You know, this house has been on the market for months. Funny your friends haven't looked at it yet.''

''Well, they don't get over to this side of town much. But I'll be sure to tell them it's shaping up nicely. For now, it'll be sealed off, anyway. Part of a murder investigation.''

''Sure.'' The painter was still frowning.

''Listen. Until the officers get here, I think I'll just walk around a bit.'' Brad stepped toward the house, pretending to peer into a bay window. ''We have a lot of ground to cover.''

The painter shrugged. ''Suit yourself. Guess I'd better start cleaning up.'' He disappeared over the edge of the parapet and Brad drew a steadying breath. The presence of the man complicated things, but the search warrant had been issued and the police were on their way. Brad had to get this bit of business done, painter on the premises or not.

He held his pace to a saunter as he made his way toward the rear of the grounds where the grotto was, but his mind whirled ahead. When he got back there, the hedge would conceal him, and then it was just a simple matter of finding the loose stone.

But when he arrived at the grotto, he suffered a disorienting jolt. The thing had been completely repaired. The large limestone that had slid forward, revealing the secret spot, was mortared in place now.

He tried not panic as his mind pawed through possibilities. Without the loose stone, which he had planned to "discover" during the search today, he would have to find another far less logical hiding place. And the clock was ticking. Frantically he looked for alternatives. Not under some bush, for crying out loud!

His eyes fastened on the flagstone path that led around the grotto, then down to the creek at the back of the mansion. *There*. One particular rock, a flat hubcap-size piece, gave with a nudge from his heel. He dropped to one knee and tipped it up against the wall of the grotto. Using his hands to dig in the earth, which was loose and surprisingly cooperative, he clawed away, cursing under his breath at this disastrous turn of events.

Maybe he wanted them to find this today and maybe he didn't. If he could devise a way to get the thing down into the wall of the grotto later, that would work better. He could establish, through contractor records, that the grotto had been repaired after Susie disappeared. He would simply subpoena all contractor records as a first step. Of course! It would appear that he was being thorough, trying to discover if Biddle had destroyed evidence by remodeling. He could make it all fit nicely.

Brad stepped up his work while birdsong and sunshine gave the illusion of a gardener—albeit one wearing a business suit—digging rapidly in a well-composted bed on a lovely fall morning. When the hole was a good foot deep, he drew the package out of his belt. Carefully he untied the twine and unrolled the cloth, holding the object by a final fold between thumb and forefinger. The thing was clean as a whistle, but, Brad reasoned, Biddle would undoubtedly have washed it as thoroughly as he himself had. *Only Biddle wouldn't have hidden it here like this.* Nevermind. He would simply have to make that aspect of it work.

The sound of someone whistling floated to him on the morning air, and Brad jumped, then reminded himself: *the painter.*

He peered through the hedge and saw the man's white-clad back high on the parapet. He was bent forward, putting tools into a box. Brad, satisfied that the man wasn't keeping track of his movements, quickly dropped his item in the hole. This would simply have to do until he could move it to the grotto. Panic would be motive enough to explain Biddle's bizarre behavior. Brad could certainly build a case for panic. He quickly scooped soil over the gleaming object. After one last backward glance, he lowered the stone. He'd certainly have to do some fast talking if this thing was discovered now, but what choice did he have? All the other evidence was circumstantial so far, but this was real physical evidence. Seen, perhaps even touched by a jury, it wouldn't necessarily convict, but it would sway them. On the heels of that thought, he heard engines, then doors slamming at the front of the mansion. He started to sweat. He had sweated every single incident, every single moment of his life almost, since that horrid night. But he would have to maintain awhile longer...

He quickly tamped the compost around the stone, scattering a few dry leaves to create what he hoped was a natural pattern. Then he scanned the sky. *Come on, baby. Rain.* Surely the old cabin had gone up in flames already; now Brad needed rain to cover his tracks here.

He sighed, stood and wiped his soiled hands on the same white cloth from which he had just unrolled Nathan Biddle's grandfather's knife.

DAVE BROUGHT the news wagon to a lurching halt right behind the squad cars. He jumped out and had the tape rolling just as three cops entered the front door of the mansion. How'd they get a key? He noticed a painter loading stuff into a van at the curb and, once the cops had gone inside, Dave swung the camera over and filmed the guy's face, the logo and the information on the side of the van. Could be useful—who knows? This way Jamie would have it.

The painter, who had spotted him doing the shoot, walked over. "Hi," he said, and Dave relaxed. The guy wasn't going to get hostile about being taped.

"Just wanted your company name and all. Hope that's okay."

"Sure. Put me on the news if you can. What do they call that? Subliminal advertising?"

Dave smiled.

"What's going on?" the painter asked.

"The Biddle murder. They've got a search warrant."

"So the guy told me. I meant, what are they looking for?"

"Not sure. What guy?"

"The one who showed up early. Skinny blond guy, running around on the back grounds. Made me pack up. Looks like rain, anyway. It'll take forever to get the old joint painted once the fall rains start. Well, good luck.''

''Thanks.'' Dave waved. He probably should have gotten more information out of that painter, but hell, he wasn't a reporter. This situation was not ideal, shooting footage without a reporter by his side to do the bullshitting, but there'd been no one available. All the general-assignment reporters were tied up with the fire. Dave knew that if Jamie could, she'd want to cover this search herself. A nasty hitch of worry seized him again as he wondered if Jamie and Biddle had escaped the fire okay. He shook it off. Jamie'd be fine. Jamie Evans was like a cat with nine lives.

A cop emerged from the house, and Dave filmed while the uniform unfurled crime-scene tape across the front door, then around the perimeter of the yard. The guy approached Dave when he'd finished the job. ''That's all you're getting, you know,'' he said smugly.

''Ah, man,'' Dave whined. ''Can't you let me have just one itty-bitty sweep of the interior? Is it creepy in there? Can't I hang around in case you find something?''

''Nope.''

''Hey, my boss didn't send me out here to film the petunias, you know.''

''Sorry.'' The cop was already walking away.

A guy in a suit came around the side of the

house and stopped in the middle of the sunny brick entry walk. He and the cop talked, casting furtive looks Dave's way.

Dave dropped the camera off his shoulder but kept it rolling on them the whole time, of course. And while the guy in the suit walked forward, waving a palm to send him away, Dave kept filming.

"Brad Alexander," the suit said as he thrust a hand forward, right at the lens of the camera at Dave's side. "First Assistant District Attorney."

"Yeah, I know. We've…met. Dave Reardon. Channel Six." Dave shook the guy's hand, which felt slightly gritty.

"Right. Listen, Dave, I'm afraid there's not much to film here. And I'm afraid I can't let you inside. Because the place has been remodeled, testing for bloodstains is going to be tricky as it is."

Dave shrugged. "That's okay. I've shot plenty of police tape in my time. Mind if I get you in the frame?" He didn't need the guy's permission, but Jamie had taught him some things about people and cooperation.

"I'd rather you didn't."

Odd, Dave thought. Political types usually clamored to be in the picture, even if they were just standing around picking their noses. "Okay," he said, and raised the camera, aiming at the front door and the twisted yellow tape. But when Brad

Alexander walked off, Dave sneaked a shot of his retreating back, anyway.

"TEST-SPRAY EVERYTHING," Brad told the detectives. "This guy's not gonna get away with murder just because he remodeled this joint."

"Back to theory one," the chief investigator grumbled, "on a three-year-old crime scene."

"Hey," Brad snapped, "Trent thinks he killed her here and moved the body to the river. Biddle was smart enough to take her over the county line so Trent couldn't go after him. But it ain't gonna work." He turned to the others working the search warrant. "As you boys know, among other things, we are looking for a large knife, possibly a hunting knife."

"Which he stashed here?" a forensic technician said. "Seems like he'd dump the thing."

"Well, he'd like for us to believe that, wouldn't he?"

"Anybody checked the grounds yet?" the homicide investigator said wearily.

Brad swiveled his head. "I'll look out there."

The investigator squinted at him. "That's my job."

"Your job is to provide the prosecutor with evidence that can be used in court. So do it."

"Baker," the gruff investigator commanded one

of his team, "go check the grounds with Mr. Alexander."

THE JANGLING PHONE woke Jamie from a desperately needed sleep. Yesterday's wildfire, wild horse, near-drowning fiasco had worn her out.

"Shut the hell up," she muttered on the third ring, but no up-and-coming reporter could afford to ignore the phone, even if it was her day off. She groped for it and mumbled, "Hullo."

"Jamie! You've been all over the news up here. Mom and Dad are beside themselves."

Valerie. Only her big sister would have the nerve to call and wake her up at—she cracked an eye at the digital clock—seven thirty-five in the morning. Undoubtedly Valerie's hubby had just left for work, the oatmeal bowls were thoroughly washed, and her three-year-old nephew was watching a kiddy show on TV. Jamie could hear the music in the background. "Good morning, Val," she croaked.

"Were you asleep or something?"

"Or something." Jamie scooted herself up on the pillows.

"You wish."

"It just so happens I have a hunk right here beside me this very minute. Masses of muscles, leather vest, big old sword—you can sheath that

thing now, honey,'' she said to her empty bedroom, "I'd rather talk to my big sister.''

Valerie chuckled. "I imagine you're way too
busy for a love life. Running from wildfires, interviewing murder suspects.''

Jamie wanted to say, *Beats diapers and bottles,*
but the truth was, actually, it didn't. "They've really run that story up there in KC?''

"Only about a half a minute. The voice-over
was mostly about you, the up-and-comer and,
might I add, even if I am your big sister, also *gorgeous* young reporter who narrowly escaped a raging wildfire on the back of a horse with a *murder
suspect.* I must say, that part really got Mom worrying—''

Undoubtedly Mom would be calling next. Jamie
bit her lip, feeling a pang of guilt for not calling
her parents to tell them she was okay.

"Don't panic, but Mom and Dad called Phil
Hooks and he told them you were fine.''

"That's good.'' Now fully awake, Jamie tossed
aside the covers and vaulted out of bed. Wait till
she told Dave that their story had made it to the
Kansas City market. The Oklahoma City stations
had picked up the story, of course. But KC! She
wondered if any stations in Dallas had run anything about it.

"You said voice-over. Was there footage?''

"Yeah. A helicopter shot of the fire. A pub

photo of you in the corner. A close-up of that man as they moved him from the squad car to the jail. I must say *he* looks pretty wild—my God, Jamie, what were you thinking, running around on a horse with a man like that?''

"It was either that or get barbecued.''

"God! Don't talk like that. I'm glad you're okay. Was it scary?''

"Not terribly. Nathan Biddle knew what to do. He actually took pretty good care of me.''

"That's the murder suspect's name? Nathan Biddle? What's he like? The news story said he's incredibly rich. Even I have to admit, he *is* awfully good-looking—for a murderer.''

"He's not a murderer, Valerie.''

Jamie didn't need anything but the abrupt silence on the other end of the line to alert her that her sister instantly sensed that something was up.

"Exactly how would you know that?''

"Call it a feeling.''

"What kind of feeling?'' The suspicion in her sister's voice came through loud and clear.

"It's too complicated to explain. Let's just say, I've been looking into this case for a long time, and something tells me—''

"Your famous instincts again?''

"Hey. I can trust my gut, okay? As a matter of fact, he saved my life thr—''

"You just be careful with your guts.''

"Three times," Jamie finished under her breath.

"I don't like the way you're talking about this guy."

"The way I'm talking?"

"Yeah. You sound as though you *like* him or *admire* him or something."

"He's a nice guy, Val. Really nice."

"You wouldn't appreciate a nice guy if he fell out of the sky and landed on your head."

"That's not fair."

"It isn't? Look how you went nuts over that Ethan creep. You certainly had a gut feeling about him, didn't you. Let's face it, you're fascinated by bad boys."

"Ethan was a long time ago."

"And then look how you dumped the decent guy. Poor Donald. That wasn't so long ago, young lady."

"Poor Donald? Listen, I gave Donald every chance in the world. Donald was an uptight jerk. Is that what you want? To see your baby sister married to some uptight jerk?"

"Heck no. But I don't want to see her getting all soft and fuzzy-headed about a murderer, either."

"I told you, he's not a murderer. I think this guy was framed. And I'm going to do everything I can to help him prove it."

"Oh, my gosh." Jamie could envision Valerie

rolling her eyes and smiting her forehead. "Jamie, do not get emotionally involved with this guy. Do you understand me? Promise me you won't do anything stupid."

"Oh, all *right*. I promise." Jamie now thoroughly irritated, added, "It's just a story, okay? I am not about to get emotionally involved with the man." But even as the words left her mouth, Jamie knew she already was involved.

No sooner had she gotten rid of Valerie than her pager sounded. She recognized the number and dialed Brad Alexander's office while she made coffee.

"What's up?" she said tiredly when he answered.

"Some smart young cop found the knife," he said.

Jamie's radar went up. Brad, it seemed to her, was dangerously generous with such late-breaking facts. Shouldn't he be worried that she would leak such information to the perpetrator? "Where?"

"The mansion. He'd buried it out back."

"That's insane."

"Nobody said this guy was normal."

"Now what?"

"Now forensics takes the knife apart, looking for old blood in the hilt. Hopefully we'll match some with Susie's DNA."

"But that still doesn't prove Nathan Biddle did anything."

"No, but it doesn't look good for him." Brad's sigh sounded theatrical. "Especially since he completely gutted and remodeled the crime scene. And now, considering where the knife was found…let's just say that Trent feels pretty confident the trial will be in Tulsa County now."

CHAPTER SEVEN

"IT'S LIKE IN THE OLD TIMES when the black crows, first one and then a gathering flock, would follow the Osage war parties out." Robert was getting breathless keeping up with Nathan as they trotted down the courthouse steps, but he was doing his best to sound like a sage, anyway.

"The crows," he went on, "knew there would be bloodshed, then feasting. After the crows came the wolves—" he drew a quick breath "—sneaking…at a distance. Then the coyotes, watching from the ridges, waiting for the kill."

Robert fanned a hand out at the crowd of media below, then at the curious onlookers behind them, all gathered in front of the Osage County courthouse to see Nathan Hart Biddle released on bond after only a few days in jail. When no one in their small party paid any attention to Robert, he intoned louder, "Crows, wolves, coyotes."

"Robert," Nathan warned as they turned onto the sidewalk and jogged away from the tangle of media, "save it."

"Yes. Save it," Nathan's lawyer, Cynthia Ridley, also heavyset and slightly breathless, echoed from his side. "Nathan, remember to keep moving. Say nothing," she said, repeating the instructions she'd given him when they left the holding cell. Nathan had been arraigned within seventy-two hours, and thanks to his family's millions and the sharp female attorney at his side, he had been released on bail the very next day.

"I wasn't planning to stop for a chat," Nathan mumbled.

"Was this not true of the ancient war parties?" Robert persisted in a singsong voice. "And now, like the ancients, we go to war."

Nathan figured his goofy cousin was employing this Native-speak for Jamie Evans's benefit. But—he glanced to his left—Jamie didn't look entertained. She was eyeing the crowd ahead as it pressed closer to them. It couldn't be fun facing her own kind from the other side. Maybe she was starting to regret coming along after he'd asked Cynthia to call her. Nathan grabbed her arm and guided her around to his back as the crowd closed in. "Get behind me," he suggested.

"Watch her back," Nathan instructed his cousin.

"Like the crows," Robert intoned as he stepped up to close the space behind Jamie. "Looking for blood."

Nathan wished he could whop Robert upside the

head. Unfortunately there were witnesses. Witnesses with cameras rolling and microphones thrust forward. Nathan put out a hand to fend off the onslaught. "No comment," he said again and again while he elbowed a path through the throng. Some of Jamie's colleagues, he noticed, gave her curious censoring looks. She planted a palm on his back, and Nathan had to struggle to keep her body positioned squarely between himself and Robert. Crowds could get ugly, even when they were wielding only cameras and microphones.

"Why did you kill your wife?" a shrill-sounding female voice pierced the cacophony.

He froze in his tracks, turned his gaze on the woman, said nothing. The reporter jerked back the mike she'd thrust forward as if Nathan had slapped it.

"Keep moving," Cynthia commanded, but Nathan, still glaring at the woman, didn't budge.

Jamie stepped around and took his arm. "Nathan. The car is waiting."

"Yes." Cynthia took his other arm. "Get to the car." Between them, they shoved him forward.

Jamie led the way around the corner of the courthouse where Dave waited behind the wheel of the Channel Six news wagon. He was fuming, no doubt about being deprived of jostling with the other cameramen to get a shot of Nathan Biddle coming down those courthouse steps. But, as Jamie had repeatedly reminded him, the other stations would run the same old suspect-leaving-the-courthouse footage, and *their* broadcast would feature a face-to-face exclusive.

There was a tense moment as they decided who should take which seat—Robert, being the largest, ducked into the passenger side, riding shotgun, and Jamie took the center back between Nathan and Cynthia. Then three doors slammed in rapid succession and the van roared away from the curb.

"Where to?" Dave called over his shoulder to Jamie.

But Nathan Biddle answered, "Owasso and Thirty-first Street."

"The Biddle mansion?" Jamie exchanged a meaningful look with Dave in the rearview mirror. An interview in Biddle's old home would make a great story but seemed somehow too much—and totally unexpected.

"It happens to be my home."

"But—"

"But I said I'd never go back?"

Jamie nodded. She'd seen him say those very words on tape in the weeks after his wife disappeared.

"That was before. Now I've decided it will be better if I'm visible."

"You mean to underscore the fact that you're innocent and have nothing to hide?"

"No. To flush out the killer."

"Nathan—" Cynthia's voice was testy as she leaned around Jamie "—I did not fight to get the cops to let you back in there so you could play vigilante."

"I told you what I want."

"And I told you that my job is to save your neck. As soon as the Grand Jury gives Trent his way, we may have only ninety days to get ready for trial."

"Then that doesn't give me much time to catch Susie's killer."

"You are not—" Cynthia scooted her bulk forward on the seat and pointed an aggressive finger at Nathan "—using yourself as some kind of human decoy. Whoever framed you isn't going to come running out of hiding just because you decide to go swaggering around Tulsa making threatening noises."

"You think he was framed?" Jamie turned her head from side to side, but didn't really expect either of them to answer, because it was a rhetorical question. The murder weapon conveniently shows up under a rock at the Biddle mansion? The real mystery was, why couldn't Trent Van Horn see the ridiculousness of this setup? Or rather, why didn't he want to?

"We're going to the mansion," Nathan said firmly. "That's where I want this interview filmed.

That's where I'll be staying until this thing is over. The ranch house is smoked and being cleaned, and Robert needs a place to stay as well."

ROBERT, IT APPEARED, had most certainly found his place to "stay" while Nathan had been in jail. Jamie recognized his messy trail the minute they stepped into the foyer: a greasy banged-up ball cap tossed on the hall table, a discarded flannel shirt lying on the small settee, muddy boots tossed on the Italian-marble tiles.

And the old dog, Bear, had made himself at home, too. He trotted up the minute they stepped through the carved double doors of Nathan Biddle's Owasso Street mansion.

She raised her eyes to fourteen-foot-high ceilings trimmed with the kind of elaborate crown moldings favored in the 1930s, when, her research had informed her, this mansion had been built. Subsequent generations had added two one-story wings to the three-story main house. Eight thousand square feet of…loneliness.

Reminding herself that the mistress of this opulent home had now been confirmed as a victim of murder, Jamie drew a fortifying breath and stepped farther inside. Her high heels made a hollow sound on the marble flooring that led to a huge winding staircase, and she felt the urge to turn on those heels and run all the way back to her own clean cozy town house in Brookside Square.

"In here," Nathan's deep voice said from behind her.

She swung around.

He stood under a double-door entryway opposite the staircase, scratching the dog's head. He extended his hand, inviting the group into the large room beyond.

Dave shot Jamie a look that said, "Creepy," as they followed Biddle inside.

Nathan crossed the hardwood flooring to a set of thick damask drapes. He found a cord and yanked them open. Flooding the room with sunlight did nothing to alleviate its sad vacant appearance. In here, too, Robert had done his dirty work. A pizza box on the table in front of marble fireplace. A CD player, tethered to a wall socket by a long extension cord, sat in the middle of a plush Persian rug, surrounded by a smattering of disks and discarded jewel cases. Robert made no apologetic attempt to clean up the mess; instead he planted himself off to one side of the room, arms folded across his bulky chest, looking for all the world like an Osage warrior stationed at the fringes of the lodge. Observant. Ominous.

Jamie cleared her throat. "Where do you think?" she said to Dave. "On the leather couch?"

"Nah. Nothing interesting in the background. I

say we pull that wing chair over next to the fireplace. You sit opposite him. Kind of do the Barbara Walters thing.''

''I'll stand right here.'' Nathan's voice made her jump. He was at the opposite wall, standing below a cluster of photographs Jamie hadn't noticed before. Photographs of his wife. It looked like a movie storyboard: *The Tale of a Happy Marriage.* Now, of course, the wall of photos looked more like a shrine. There were flawless studio portraits of each of them separately and as a couple; trophy shots of them with famous political or entertainment figures; photos of them receiving awards, shaking hands; snapshots of their various adventures—scuba diving, horseback riding, river rafting.

''Oh, I don't know...'' Jamie looked to Dave for support. ''Do you think that background clutter will film all that well?'' She didn't want this kind of emotion, this kind of biased image to appear in the story.

''I'll stand right *here,*'' Nathan repeated, pointing at the floor, ''or the interview is off.''

At the fierce look in his eyes, Jamie swallowed, then nodded. Normally she wouldn't allow a subject to stage the shot. But this was no ordinary subject. They weren't doing a profile of some political candidate. They were telling the story of a murder—and this was the prime suspect.

"Okay. A stand-up shot. That might be more immediate, more dramatic, anyway." But a stand-up also meant she would get less out of the subject than if he were sitting, relaxed, on that leather couch. Dave opened the tripod, and she walked over to stand beside Nathan.

He removed his cowboy hat, and without being coached either way, he turned his eyes lovingly toward the pictures. Dave was already rolling, had been, Jamie knew, since they'd walked into the house.

"I will find out who killed my wife or die trying," Nathan vowed, seeming to wince at the images.

Sound bite.

"Do you have any idea who that might be, Mr. Biddle?" Jamie wanted to signal him that the interview had started, although this man—unlike the Trent Van Horns of the world—apparently didn't care whether there was an audience or not. Nothing about his demeanor changed as he continued speaking, his voice almost trancelike. "I haven't the slightest idea who would want to hurt a gentle person like Susie, but I *will* find out." His eyes moved to the camera, and Dave zoomed in. "If it's the last thing I do."

Sound bite.

Tears, Jamie thought, seemed to be forming in the depths of those eyes, and for some reason Jamie touched Dave's arm, signaling him to stop the camera, something she would never do in an ordinary interview.

"Nathan," she said softly as she stepped toward him. "Maybe we should do this interview another time. We can come back after you've had a chance to rest, to absorb everything that's happened."

Jamie caught Dave's sidelong glance and frown. She couldn't explain her decision even to herself. Except that her pounding heart warned her not to betray Nathan's trust, not to hurt him. And once again, her heart told her that this man was no killer.

"No." Nathan turned his head toward the pictures again. "Turn the camera on. Ask me anything. You have to remember, I've done this many times before."

"But not when you've just been charged—"

"I don't care about that," he said quietly. "Maybe this will help somehow. You know, force the killer to make a move. Threaten him."

"Okay," Jamie said shakily, signaling Dave to begin again, then she strengthened her voice for the tape. "Mr. Biddle, tell me what you know about your grandfather's knife. The one they found."

Behind her, she heard Robert make a sound—a small grunt of disapproval, disgust or…anger?

"That knife may have been the one that injured my wife, but it wasn't in my hand at the time."

Sound bite.

The doorbell chimed, startling them all. The puzzled look in Nathan's eyes said he wasn't expecting company.

But before he reached the door, a thick-set man and a pencil-thin blond woman swooped into the room. Their clothing was casual, but obviously expensive.

"Hunter? Andrea?" Nathan seemed surprised, though relieved, to see the couple.

"Nathan!" the woman cried as she crossed the room with arms outstretched. "Sorry to barge in, but the door was unlocked—"

"And we saw the Channel Six van out front." The man gave Jamie a frown. "We've been worried sick about you, man. We came as soon as we heard you were out of jail." The man grabbed Nathan in a bear hug. "Hang in there, buddy." Over Nathan's shoulder, his gaze became hostile as he took in Jamie, Dave and the camera.

"Robert, sweetie. How are you holding up?" the woman said.

"All right." Robert gave her a stoic nod.

"I'm Hunter Roth, and this is my wife Andrea. We live around the corner—longtime friends of Nathan's." The man stuck out his hand as he continued to assess Jamie.

"I'm Jamie Evans and this Dave Reardon."

As they all shook hands, Hunter said, "From

Channel Six? I must say, you television types never stop digging for more.''

''My God—'' the woman turned on Jamie ''—can't you people leave him in peace for one single minute?'' It seemed to Jamie that the Roths were either awfully protective of Nathan...or awfully hostile toward the media.

Nathan spoke up. ''I asked Ms. Evans to come here.''

''Oh,'' Hunter and Andrea said at the same time.

Then the duo turned away from Jamie and Dave and focused their attention squarely on Nathan.

''Susie's body, that fire, getting arrested!'' Andrea spread her palm on her flat chest. ''It's all too much, Nathan!''

''Is there somewhere private we can talk, Nathan?'' Hunter took his wife's elbow.

''I'm not keeping secrets from Ms. Evans. She's going to help me find Susie's killer.''

''Nathan.'' Hunter narrowed his eyes at Jamie, as if she was a spy for the bad guys. ''Are you sure that's wise?''

''I'm positive.''

There wasn't enough seating in the barren great room, so they all moved to the dining room, where Robert had left his messy mark yet again. How, Jamie wondered, had one man created such chaos in the few short days that Nathan had been in jail? They shoved aside the empty soda cans, unfolded laundry and newspapers, and seated themselves at the table. To their credit, Hunter and Andrea seemed unfazed by the mess.

"Looks like Teddy and Cassie have been through here."

Nathan smiled fondly at Hunter. "And how are the twins?"

"Spoiled."

"Impossible."

Hunter and Andrea had spoken in unison again, but their delighted smiles belied their droll description of their children.

Nathan asked to see pictures, and Andrea produced the latest school shots from her wallet.

Jamie looked, then passed the photos on politely. "They're darling," she said, smiling at the mother. And they were. Robust. Freckle-faced. The kind of children that had probably kept Nathan and Susie Biddle dreaming throughout their frustrating struggles with infertility.

"A darn sight better-looking than their old man," Nathan kidded.

"Their mother's genes saved them." Hunter grinned.

"No doubt. Which makes them a darn sight smarter than their old man, too." Nathan winked at Andrea.

"Which actually isn't saying much," Hunter added.

Jamie had the impression that Hunter, bespectacled and soft around the edges, was a man who earned his living with his brains. A lawyer, maybe? A stockbroker? Or perhaps he was in the oil-and-gas business, too.

Nathan chuckled with Hunter, but Jamie had seen the sadness in his eyes as he studied the pictures of the alert healthy young faces.

"I must have them out to the ranch for some horseback riding," he said as he handed the photos back to the children's mother.

"What an excellent idea!" Andrea beamed.

"We'd never get Cassie off that ranch!" Hunter put in.

"When this is over..." Nathan's voice trailed off.

"Yes. When this is over."

"When this is over."

The atmosphere grew subdued and the couple fixed their concerned gazes on Nathan.

"Have you retained an attorney?" Hunter asked.

"Cynthia Ridley."

"From Fitch and Baker?" Hunter confirmed. "That's good."

"She's top-notch, I hear," Andrea chimed in.

"What happens next?" Hunter wanted to know.

"I'll have a preliminary hearing within ten days."

"And after that, will you be going back to the ranch?"

"No. I'm staying here."

"But...but won't that...*expose* you?" Andrea bit her lip and sent a blaming glance Jamie's way.

"Exposure is the idea."

For the first time in the conversation, Robert spoke. "My cousin has nothing to hide."

"Of course, he doesn't," Hunter shot back. "We are concerned for him, that's all. Remember what the publicity did to his life when...last time?"

"I can handle it." Nathan smiled at Hunter.

"Nathan—" Andrea's voice had deepened with concern "—we can understand why you would want to prove your innocence, but to remain so visible when—"

"It's not about proving my innocence," Nathan interrupted her. "I'm not out to clear my name. I'm here to find Susie's killer."

"I see," Andrea breathed.

Hunter bit his lip and frowned. "And you think the killer is here in Tulsa?"

"Don't you? The police and the FBI, back before they decided I was their man, said the killer is usually someone the victim knows, or at least someone who knows of the victim."

The couple exchanged a look and clasped hands.

"In Susie's case—" Hunter cleared his throat "—that could be half the town."

"Nathan, we—" Andrea began, but Jamie caught the husband's warning squeeze of his wife's hand. "Nathan," Andrea began again, "we just want you to know that we're here to support you no matter what."

"Yes," Hunter said. "Is there anything at all we can do to help you?"

"Yeah." Nathan smiled and raked a hand through his wild thick hair. "Do you guys know where I can get a decent haircut on short notice?"

NATHAN GOT THE HAIRCUT—business short—rented a Mercedes and started wearing the Tulsa preppy uniform—chinos, golf shirts, tassel loafers—around town. Jamie hardly recognized him, when she saw him two weeks later.

He was wearing a tuxedo.

And she was wearing a strapless ice-pink ball gown with a graceful chiffon skirt that made her waist look tiny and a fitted sequined bodice that made her bust look full.

They stared at each other from across an elegantly decorated room filled with Tulsa matrons and patrons, movers and shakers. Nathan was flanked by Hunter and Andrea Roth. Obviously he couldn't show up at this event with a date. But the fact that he'd even shown his face at Paint the

Town, Tulsa's premier fund-raiser for children's arts, demonstrated enormous courage.

"What the hell is he doing here?" Jamie's date, Hugh Marshall, drew closer to her side. Something about Hugh—that cloying aftershave?—bothered Jamie a little more each time they went out.

She leaned away. In fact, Hugh's whole attitude had begun to bug her lately. The man was always one snipe away from a quarrel. A lawyer who thought he was the final authority on everything, Hugh delighted in arguing his point, and Jamie delighted in setting him back on his pompous ass. They were a bad mix, and Jamie decided right then and there that she wouldn't be accepting any more dates with Hugh, no matter how much her boss pressured her to be seen around town, no matter how dearly she wanted to wear a dress like this one.

"That man is an accused murderer," Hugh informed their cluster of acquaintances, as if Jamie hadn't been talking about the case on TV for weeks.

"He happens to be free on bail," Jamie countered, "and innocent until proven guilty."

"Nevertheless he shouldn't be here."

"He's one of the original founders of this event."

"Stop defending him!"

"Stop attacking him!"

The faces of the couples around them registered flickers of embarrassment.

"Would you excuse me?" she said to the group. "I think I'll go say hello."

As she approached Nathan and the Roths, Nathan's eyes shone approvingly, admiring the dress, her bare shoulders, her hair—pulled gracefully up off her neck to show off long rhinestone earrings. "I take it you're not working," he said quietly when she was close enough to hear.

"No. I'm here as a civilian."

He gave her a wry smile, which deepened his dimple on one side. Good Lord, the man was beyond handsome. His teeth were whiter than snow and his hair—slicked back—shone like a crow's wing.

"Don't you look *wonderful!*" Hunter gushed at Jamie.

"Ms. Evans, it's nice to see you again," Andrea said as if she wasn't so sure and then immediately added, "Nathan, shouldn't we find our table?" Her eyes scanned the crowd for allies.

"A different Channel Six reporter is covering this event," Jamie explained to Nathan, and pointed to the corner where media cameras, tripods, mikes, and the people who knew how to use them were setting up.

"Are you here with Hugh Marshall?" Nathan asked.

Jamie nodded. "A type of penance."

Another wry grin.

Andrea's mouth made a disapproving little "O" at Jamie's quip, which she quickly changed into a tight polite smile. "And how is Hugh?" she said.

"Fine. Said he'd love to visit you, but I don't know where he's disappeared to." Jamie craned her neck.

"There he is." Andrea grabbed Hunter's arm. "Nathan, don't you want to come and say hi to Hugh?"

"Why don't we fetch the drinks?" Nathan suggested with a toggle of his index finger from himself to Jamie.

"Good idea." Jamie tilted her head and smiled at him.

"White wine, sweetheart?" Hunter said, already digging out cash.

But Nathan stopped him. "I'll take care of it."

Hunter gave him a grudging smile. "Gin and tonic for me, then."

"We'll see you at table twelve. Thanks, Nathan," Andrea said. She and Hunter took off in Hugh's direction.

Nathan hooked his palm lightly under Jamie's elbow, and she felt an instant thrill. As they crossed the crowded room to the bar, people stared, then smiled, at both of them. Jamie didn't care what anyone thought, and she hoped Nathan didn't, either. In fact, she hoped he was as excited by this serendipitous meeting as she was.

"Nathan!" an older man cried. "It's great to see you!" A standard greeting, but delivered with enough genuine enthusiasm to imply other meanings, like, *Good for you!* and *We support you!*

"Martin, how are you?" Nathan and the gentleman shook hands.

The silver-haired, sweet-faced matron at the man's side squeezed Nathan's forearm and he bent and kissed her cheek. "Mary, dear."

"Martin and Mary Putnam, I'd like you to meet Jamie Evans."

"It's nice to meet you." Jamie smiled.

"We know who Jamie is." Mary's answering smile was friendly enough, although Jamie detected a hint of wariness. "We watch her every night."

"Me, too," Nathan said simply. The gaze he turned on Jamie was warm with affection.

He watches me every night? Jamie felt her heartbeat speed up. Even more startling was his willingness to admit it in front of these people.

"How are you holding up?" Martin leaned toward Nathan.

"We won't talk about that now," Mary chastised. "Nathan is having a night out."

Martin gave his wife a tolerant grimace. "I expect he can't think about anything else."

"I've decided it's best to be visible," Nathan explained.

"Right. You've got nothing to hide," Martin said.

"You mustn't stay away any longer, Nathan." Mary touched her fingers to his sleeve. "This will pass. And Tulsa will be waiting for you with open arms when it does."

"And we'll kick that nincompoop DA all the way across the state line come spring," Martin added.

Jamie decided these people must be wealthy, powerful and courageous to be talking about Van Horn this way.

"We've got some people waiting for their drinks," Nathan said brightly. "It was great to see you two."

"Call us, Nathan—when you can." Mary's eyes were sad now.

"I will."

They didn't stop to chat again. Nathan was a master at the nod-and-pass technique.

"So, what's with you and Hugh?" Nathan said when they had the drinks in hand.

"Convenience." Jamie sipped her wine.

"I see."

But Jamie was afraid he misunderstood. "On-camera reporters are expected to appear at community stuff. He's just a date."

"Then he won't care if I ask you to dance?"

Jamie almost spilled the drinks she was carrying. The image of Nathan and Susie, waltzing expertly at events like this, flashed through her mind. More than once they had commanded the spotlight.

"I'm not a great dancer," she hedged.

"Then we're a match. I'm no great dancer, either. I've been on the back of a horse for three years. So, is it yes or no?"

Jamie stopped and took a gulp of her wine. She wanted to dance with him in the worst way. "Yes," she said quickly.

Andrea and Hunter were settled with another couple at table twelve, which was tucked in a corner decorated with fiscus trees and tiny white lights. Hunter and the other man had already amassed piles of hors d'oeuvres on their plates. Hugh was nowhere in sight.

"Food's great!" Hunter said as he reached for his drink.

"We're going to go ahead and dance," Nathan informed his friends before Jamie could take a seat.

Jamie swallowed, wanting to toss back the glass of wine to give herself courage. But he took it from her hand and set it on the table, then offered her his arm.

Dancing with Nathan Biddle proved to be a lesson in surrender and grace.

Before he even started, he said, "Just relax, and

let's see what my feet remember." He took her slender hand lightly in his large one, then splayed a warm palm against her back.

The band, a large stage combo, specialized in instrumentals of Broadway show tunes. Currently they were playing a smooth lazy rendition of "On the Street Where You Live."

Jamie, who'd always had a tendency to gallop around with her dance partners like an awkward young filly, found herself floating like a butterfly in this man's arms. He had lied, of course. He was a great dancer.

"You are very beautiful," he said as he guided her in a confident, gentle waltz. Though he maintained a respectful distance between them, suddenly their pose felt intimate. Jamie stared over his shoulder, tempted to strain back from him. But when he felt her tense, he held her all the more lightly, and that seemed more sexual than if he'd ground his pelvis against hers. "You okay?" he asked.

"Of course. We're only dancing." *And you just told me I'm beautiful.*

"You dance very well. Maybe that's why people are staring at us."

She shot a look at his face. He had that crooked grin again, and a teasing arched eyebrow. She laughed nervously. "Aren't you afraid of anything?"

"Of course. But I'm not afraid of what these people think. Are you?"

"No. Not of these people."

"Who, then?"

"Never mind. I asked you first. What are you afraid of?"

His eyes, already black as onyx, flashed even darker. "That I won't ever find the killer."

"Of course," she whispered. "I'm sorry I asked."

Suddenly he held her tighter. "Don't be. Let me be honest with you. I'm also afraid that when this is over, I'll never see you again."

Jamie didn't know how to answer that. His admission stunned her for one thing. She knew they were attracted to each other. Only a fool would think otherwise, but to speak openly of any kind of future between them…she wasn't ready for that. Too much was hanging in the balance.

The band continued a medley of love songs which flowed into "People Will Say We're In Love" from the musical "Oklahoma." The tune—traditional fare at Oklahoma charity balls—needed no lyrics for Jamie to feel its implication. She stiffened again.

Nathan could have released her, but he didn't. He drew her an inch closer and hummed close to her ear, "Mmm… Darling, they're suspecting…"

Jamie leaned back and checked his expression: a dimpled smirk. Maybe he thought this was funny but she didn't.

She was saved by Hugh, who chose that precise moment to cut in.

Hugh, being Hugh, was not exactly courtly about the exchange, but Nathan was.

"Thank you, Jamie," he said, giving her a little bow. "That was one of the nicest experiences I've had in a long time."

Then he turned and disappeared into the crowd. Jamie did not see him again that evening, partly thanks to Hugh's possessive navigation, and she suspected Nathan and the Roths had departed early. And that disappointed her greatly.

THE NEXT TIME she saw Nathan, a week later, his behavior wasn't nearly so suave. She had dragged Dave to the Polo Grill in Utica Square between the five-o'clock and ten-o'clock broadcasts. They were on their way to shoot a fluff piece of people at the state fair at night, eating funnel cakes and Indian tacos. "I've got to have a decent meal before I smell all that gross fair food," Jamie said as Dave opened the door to the upscale restaurant for her.

Dave rolled his eyes as they stepped inside the dark, English-style pub where the food—pricey steaks and select wines—was served in a refined atmosphere with white table cloths, brass fixtures and aged wood. "You're buying, right?"

They were invited to wait in the bar until a table was ready. As soon as they scooted up onto their barstools, Jamie noticed Brad Alexander, alone, nursing a drink at a small corner table near the fireplace.

"Look who's here." Jamie jerked her head in Brad's direction.

"Think your source has anything new?" Dave tugged on his earring and raised two fingers at the bartender for a couple of beers.

"Let him finish his drink first."

But Brad had already spotted her. "Ms. Evans!" he called. "Come join me, won't you?"

She gave Dave a how-can-I-refuse? shrug and hopped off her stool.

"Ah, and here is the ever-present cameraman," Brad said with a smirk when Dave slid down to follow.

"I'm a photojournalist," Dave muttered in Jamie's ear.

She smiled. "Behave."

"I didn't recognize you without your...props." Brad, who looked like he'd downed more than one scotch-and-soda, eyed Dave as if he wished he'd go away. "Sit down." He angled the table out from the padded bench built against the paneled wall. Jamie and Dave squeezed onto it, side by side.

Brad eased back down into his chair, folded his hands around his drink and eyed Jamie. He leaned forward. "I suppose you are aware of what's being released later this week?"

Jamie *didn't* know, but she arched an eyebrow and said nothing. It was amazing how nobody could tolerate a silence these days, how people would spill their guts just to fill an uncomfortable one.

"The final results of Susan Biddle's autopsy. I'm afraid Mr. Biddle is definitely our man."

"Oh." Jamie glanced at Dave, and the understanding passed between them that the cotton-candy-at-the-fair story had just become a dead puppy.

"Her neck had definitely been broken. No surprise there." Brad stared into his drink, then downed a huge gulp. "Question is, how'd he do it? Could have pushed her off that balcony—you know, the one where Mrs. Petree saw them fighting."

Jamie leaned forward and was about to ask him if the broken neck had been positively established as the cause of death when movement near the door caught her eye. Two large men entered the small waiting area. One of them—in a black blazer, stylish tie, white shirt and tan slacks that made him look as polished as any TV anchor—was Nathan Biddle.

"Now this is getting interesting," Dave murmured.

They watched Nathan approach the hostess podium and say something. Then he looked Jamie's way, and his gaze, glittering in the candlelit room, locked briefly with hers before spearing Alexander. Then he said something to his companion and started walking toward their corner.

The man behind him, a tall white-haired guy of about sixty, grabbed the sleeve of Nathan's wool blazer, but Nathan wrenched away.

"Of all times to be without my camera," Dave whispered as Nathan wove through the tables, bearing down on Brad Alexander like a wolf stalking its prey.

"You tell Trent Van Horn—" he aimed a finger in Brad's face before the younger man had even managed to stand up "—that he'd better stop flashing his pretty face all over TV and get out there and hunt down my wife's murderer."

"We've already found him, and you know it." Brad's voice was wavery but hostile, and he actually flinched when Nathan leaned in. "Our investigators—"

"Your *investigators?*" Nathan spat out the words. "Frank Stiles here—" Nathan jerked a thumb at the man who had walked up behind him

"—has found out more in two weeks than your ignoramus *investigators* have in three solid years."

"Really? Frank Stiles?" Brad leaned forward, addressing the man behind Nathan. "I thought you went out to pasture eons ago. Once a cop, always a cop, huh?"

"Nathan, this isn't the place," the older man said mildly, ignoring Brad's dig.

But Brad persisted. "If you have evidence, you'd better have your attorney contact my office immediately. Because in a couple of months, we go to trial." Brad pointed a threatening finger at Nathan. "And then you, sir," he said, trying—unsuccessfully—to stand up behind the table, "will pay for your crimes."

Nathan leaned over him and Brad slid back down into his chair. "Which means whoever killed my wife *won't* pay—"

"Nathan. Not *here*," the white-haired gentleman insisted.

Nathan straightened and jerked his head once, like a stallion being reined in. Then his black eyes, flashing in the light from the hurricane candle on the table, focused on Jamie. He did nothing to disguise his anger. "You're right," he said to Stiles. "What's the point of talking to these people? Here or anywhere."

Jamie felt her cheeks grow hot, and she wondered if Nathan noticed her color rising in the dim lighting. But dammit, she didn't have anything to be embarrassed about. Still, she felt trapped, her source on one side and Nathan Biddle on the other. She wanted to explain to Nathan right then and there what she was doing. She could only imagine how this looked to him, and her heart sank at the prospect of what he must be thinking. But she couldn't say one word now, not with Brad looking on. Phil Hooks, the station manager, had just today given her grief because she was getting too personally involved with her subject. If Brad sensed that, too, he'd dry up.

The man Nathan had called Frank Stiles, his private investigator she assumed, said, "Come on," and Nathan allowed himself to be led back toward the hostess podium. The tiny blonde there, all of nineteen, was wide-eyed from witnessing the scene. She stared up at Nathan, swallowed, then nodded quickly when Frank said, "Any table will do. Smoking's fine." She pasted on a smile and fumbled for two menus. Nathan followed her into the dining area, never looking back.

As soon as they were out of earshot, Brad took a swig of his drink and said, "The judge shoulda kept that guy locked up. I told you he was dangerous. He's a crazy Indian, you know."

JAMIE AND DAVE left the Polo Grill without eating. Dave grumbled about missing out on his free steak, but when they got to the fair, Jamie bought him a loaded chili dog as a peace offering. Dave kept wanting to get artsy with angle shots from up on the Ferris wheel, but Jamie was in no mood. "Shoot five close-ups of gooey fair food and then get five interesting-looking people to stuff the same in their mouths."

"That's staging."

"Oh, who cares? It's the stupid state fair, not a war. I'll put together a snappy feel-good piece that'll make the producers happy."

When they were finished and Jamie didn't turn the TV news wagon back in the direction of the station, Dave said, "Where do you think you're going?"

"The Biddle mansion. I want to know what his private eye found out."

Dave groaned. "How do you know he's even there?"

"If he isn't, he's got a cell phone. I'll track him down somehow."

"How do you know he'll talk to us? He didn't look too happy to see you schmoozing with Alexander."

"I wasn't schmoozing."

"But you're afraid Nathan Biddle thinks you were. I could see it in your eyes, girl."

"Look, I can talk to Alexander or anybody else

I want to. It's my job. Nathan Biddle doesn't own me.''

"Right. Listen. Quite frankly I am sick to death of shooting close-ups of Nathan Biddle's handsome face every time I turn around. You are not going to get the public to fall in love with this guy just because you have.''

"Would you shut up.''

"Hey. It's true. You can be straight with me.''

Jamie whipped the van onto the shoulder. "I'll cover the Biddle thing alone,'' she declared.

"Suit yourself.''

But while she did a U-turn in traffic, Dave said, "Jamie, come on now. It's getting late. Don't do anything stupid.''

She kept on driving until she wheeled the van into the back lot at Channel Six where she braked and said, "Out.''

"What about the fair piece?'' Dave protested.

"You fix it. I gave you plenty of material—stand-ups, voice-overs, sound bites. Be creative.''

Dave shrugged and reached into the back seat for the camera. "I'll keep that,'' she said. Jamie had shot her own footage before, when she worked in a smaller market. Dave shrugged again and extracted his tape, then slammed the van door. Jamie roared off into the night.

CHAPTER EIGHT

As she pulled onto Owasso Street, Jamie imagined the van with its Channel Six logo emblazoned on the sides sitting smack in the middle of the circle drive in front of the Biddle mansion, and wished she'd thought to drive her little Miata, instead. In the wake of all the recent publicity, Nathan's neighbors had become more curious than ever, and the last thing she wanted was the Roths or some other busybodies barging in during this crucial interview or talk or whatever it was going to be.

She parked on a side street and walked up the tree-darkened sidewalk, lugging the heavy camera on one side and her tote of reporter paraphernalia on the other.

As she rounded the corner, she heard the patter of rain on the canopy of trees and within seconds, it turned into a downpour. Jamie hoisted the tote higher on her shoulder and pulled her collar up as she dashed up the sidewalk. By the time she made it to the mansion steps, her chic taupe jacket was pocked with dark spots, and her hair was matted and sticking to her face. Oh, well. She wasn't going to film herself. She pushed the doorbell, waited while it completed its chimes, then rang again.

She was about to give up after the third try when he answered.

The tie and black blazer were gone. He stood there in the chandelier light, white shirtsleeves rolled up, unbuttoned collar revealing tanned throat and curls of dark hair. He filled his chest with a deep breath. "Jamie?" he said on the exhale.

"May I come in?"

He frowned and nodded, and she stepped inside, dripping onto the foyer rug.

"It's raining," she said unnecessarily.

"Hold on." He disappeared into a door at the back of the hall and reappeared with a snowy-white face towel.

"Thanks." She took it and patted her damp face. Her heavy on-camera makeup from the five-o'clock broadcast left an orangy smear on the towel. She didn't want to think about how wretched she probably looked. She censored herself for having vain thoughts when this man had such grave problems. He didn't give a damn how she looked.

"You're here about that little scene at the Polo?" he said simply.

"I want to talk...to explain."

"What's to explain? Alexander's your source, right?"

Jamie nodded, feeling inexplicably ashamed. Every time she was alone with this man, she got the same feelings. Feelings of safety and trust and...*rightness,* but then Brad Alexander would show up with his smooth convincing style, slipping her newsworthy tidbits, building the case, bearing weighty evidence, and she'd find herself starting to wonder if Nathan Biddle really was the murderer. Her doubts increased when her stupid sister brought up her past lack of judgment concerning men. Or her station manager got all over her about objectivity.

Nathan's display of open hostility tonight didn't exactly dispel her concerns. But then, she asked herself, who wouldn't be hostile toward a DA who was letting the creep who killed his wife escape?

She looked around cautiously. "Is Robert here?"

"No."

Jamie couldn't decide if that was good or bad. A chill ran through her at the thought of being alone with Nathan in this huge house. Not because she was afraid of him. If she was afraid of anything, it was her own strong feelings of attraction. She'd dreamed of him every single night since they'd danced at the Paint the Town ball.

Nathan reached around and took the heavy camera from her hand. He checked to make sure the thing was really off, then said, "You look chilled. Come in. I've built a fire."

She followed him into a small study. Unlike the other rooms in the house, this one did not look barren, abandoned. It looked lived in. A heavy mahogany desk, its surface cluttered with papers, dominated a corner where coffee-colored velvet drapes were drawn over floor-to-ceiling windows. Above these, two identical arched windows rose, bare to the stormy sky.

Next to a comfortable-looking leather chair a tall stack of large books listed crookedly. She couldn't make out the titles in the dim light. Only the fire, a real fire—no imitation gas logs for Nathan Biddle—and three large pillar candles on a massive coffee table were lit. She noted the scraps of paper sticking out of some of the books, and a yellow legal pad scribbled with notes. He took one giant step forward and turned the pad over.

"Were you...reading?" Jamie asked as she slipped her tote off her shoulder and settled herself onto the sectional leather sofa facing the fire. Even in the dim light, she could see the rich details, comfort and style of the room's rugs, lamps, throw pillows.

"No. Just thinking." Nathan set her camera next to her feet.

"This is an interesting room." Jamie's gaze

traveled up to where dozens of black-and-white photographs in coordinated frames sat propped atop a deep crown-molding ledge that ran all the way around the room.

"My ancestors," Nathan volunteered. "She arranged them that way."

With a fresh pang of sympathy, Jamie suddenly understood exactly why he had moved to the ranch. Every detail of this house probably had Susan's touch and must have reminded him of her. She supposed he still loved her. Realizing that made Jamie a little jealous. And realizing *that* made her a little sad. How absurd—to fall for a man who was a murder suspect and also still in love with the victim.

"Let me have that wet jacket." He stepped around behind her and peeled it away from her shoulders carefully, gently.

As she tilted her body and wriggled her arms free, Jamie was aware again, most keenly, of the sheer size and magnetism of the man. It was the same feeling she'd had when they'd been on the back of that horse running from the wildfire. The same feeling she'd had when he held her in his arms as they danced. And that feeling was more than simple sexual attraction, that was for sure. It felt like…something inevitable.

"Would you like some cognac?" He arranged the jacket on the back of a chair and moved to a beveled-glass hutch against one wall. He took out a small snifter that matched the one on the coffee table containing a small measure of dark-amber liquid. "Or do you have to go back on the air at ten?" He checked his watch.

"That depends on what you tell me."

"I see. Another interview?" He crossed to the table and splashed a finger of cognac into his snifter.

"Not an interview. I told you I just want to talk."

"Talk, huh?" He walked over to stand beside the fireplace, away from her. A silence filled the room while rain strafed the tall windows. A log on the fire hissed and popped, tumbling free of the others.

"Yes, talk." Jamie's eyes traveled over her dim surroundings. "Can we turn on a lamp or something?" She could almost feel the ghost of the dead woman in the corners of the room.

"No." He took a swig of the cognac.

Okay. So he was brooding. Jamie had worked in unsettling conditions before: devastating tornado wreckage, chaotic emergency rooms, fringe militia compounds. She reminded herself that she was here to extract some important information. "What did your private eye find out?"

He grimaced into his snifter. "I do wish you'd come to point occasionally, Ms. Evans."

Jamie bit her lip. They were back to *Ms. Evans?* Was he distancing himself because he'd seen her with the enemy? "Jamie. After all, we've traded spit, remember?"

He looked puzzled.

"When you pulled me from the river."

He smiled faintly and shook his head.

"So are you going to tell me?"

"Why don't you ask your friend Brad after he uncovers it?"

"You knew I had a source," she challenged. "Who did you think it was—your garbage man?"

"The problem is, I don't think *you* know who your source is."

"Is there something about Brad you think I should know?"

He glanced over his shoulder, raised an eyebrow and nodded slowly, but didn't answer her question.

"Nathan, please. I'm on your side—"

"Except when you're talking to Brad."

"Stop it."

Bee-bee-bee-beep. From her belt, Jamie's pager bleated. She grabbed it, frowning at the message. "It's the station. Excuse me."

She rummaged around in her shoulder bag, flipped open her cell phone, punched one button and said, "Jamie here."

She shot Nathan a glance and turned away, cupping the cell with her hand, covering the conversation.

Nathan turned his back and focused his attention on the flames.

"I'm lookin' at him," he heard her mutter. "Yes, I'm *fine*." There was irritation in her voice, and Nathan assumed the folks at the station knew she was alone with him in this house—and they probably didn't like it. "No. Can't Jason take the live shot?" She lowered her voice even further, but Nathan's hearing was excellent. "There's been a development in this story. I'm in the middle of an interview here."

He glanced over his shoulder. *Not an interview, huh?* She was twisted up like a pretzel on the edge of the couch. He took a second to admire her sinuous legs. He hadn't been able to take his eyes off her at the ball the other night. That was why he'd left early. He didn't want people talking about how the accused murderer had stared at the pretty TV reporter all night.

She jammed her delicate fingers through her damp hair. It seemed as if every time he was alone with this woman, she was wet. His mouth twisted in a wry smile, which quickly softened with genuine affection. Being a reporter must be tough, but she certainly seemed to handle it well. She knew how to craft the stories that demanded airtime. And for that reason she was useful to him.

Okay. He'd give the girl her interview. What did he have to lose? Unless she leaked something that would put the killer one step ahead of him and Frank. But he could control the situation, revealing only what he wanted her to know, and she, in turn, might tell him something crucial that would help him find the killer. She was awfully sharp. And the truth was, he didn't exactly want to run her off. Tonight, especially, he was glad she was here. He checked out her legs again.

She finished her conversation and punched the phone off. "They won't bother us again. Now. What did your private eye uncover?"

"Is this on the record or not?"

In other words, are you going to run to Brad with this? Jamie had to put this subtle mistrust to rest. She wanted them to be able to work together. "Look. I said it's not an interview. I was just getting my producer off my back. Okay?"

He gave her a hard stare, then scrubbed a hand over his face. "Okay, here's the deal. My private investigator, the man who was with me at the Polo Grill tonight—"

"Frank Stiles. A retired cop, right?"

She didn't miss a detail. "Yeah. A good one. He tracked down some bait-shop owner in the town of Osage—"

"That's not far from where her body was found."

His eyes hooded. "Right. This bait-shop guy re-members renting a boat to a nervous young man about three years ago."

"Good memory! Why hasn't the law found this bait-shop owner before now?"

"Apparently they have. And they're convinced the man he rented a boat to is me."

Jamie looked crestfallen. "Oh, no."

Nathan nodded, his mouth twisting ruefully.

"What makes them think that?"

"This dude was about my build, wearing sun-glasses, a Hart Ranch cap and...my signature leather jacket."

"The one with the brand stitched over the breast pocket?" Jamie remembered it well. After all, she'd pressed her face against it when he'd pulled her from the creek.

"Yep."

"But how?"

"That's the sixty-four-million-dollar question. To my knowledge that jacket never leaves its peg in the barn except when I put it on."

Jamie shook her head. She couldn't believe this. Someone wearing Nathan's jacket had rented a boat to take out on the Arkansas River around the time Susan Biddle disappeared. It didn't make sense. But somehow it had to.

"The night Susie disappeared. Tell me again *ex-actly* what happened."

"It was late when I turned my car around, somewhere up in Kansas. When I got home, Susie was gone. Her car was in the garage, her sweater was still lying right there on that couch." He pointed to Jamie's left.

She inched a bit to the right, wishing again that he'd turn on a lamp.

"There was no note, but her purse was gone. I waited about an hour, called the ranch. Then I decided to drive out there myself."

"Why?"

"Because she went out there sometimes."

"What happened when you got to the ranch?"

"No sign of her. I knew she had to be with somebody, because her car was still at the mansion, but I couldn't imagine who. An abduction crossed my mind, of course, but...the purse. And our house in Tulsa had been all locked up."

"Yeah. What kind of kidnapper would give their victim time to fetch her purse and then lock all the doors?"

"And set the alarm." His eyes closed slightly again. "We never did find that purse."

"I know," she said sadly.

"Finally I called the law."

"When was that?"

"I don't know. It seemed like I wasn't at the ranch long before the sun started coming up."

"Why did you wait so long?"

He shot her a look as if weighing whether to reveal what was on his mind. He let out a huge sigh and stared back into the fire. "She'd done it before."

"Disappeared in the middle of the night?"

He nodded. "Whenever she was upset."

"Did you tell the police that?"

He shook his head.

"Why not?"

"I... Whenever she'd leave like that, it was always impulsive, crazy. She couldn't help herself. She didn't mean it. What good would it do her family—they adored her—to know that their daughter had been so troubled?"

"But now? Have you told your attorney?"

"No."

"Nathan! For heaven's sake, why not? This is important! Maybe there's a way to find out where she went when she disappeared all those other times. Maybe that will lead us to the killer. You've *got* to share that information."

He shot her a fierce look, his eyes blazing the same way they had in the Polo Grill. "No."

"Why?"

"I told you. Susie's parents, who have suffered enough in this mess, would die if they knew how distraught their daughter was at times."

"Distraught?"

"Because of...because we couldn't get pregnant. Susie had a dramatic streak. She'd grab her purse and take off. But she always came back. She claimed she just drove around aimlessly until she felt calmer. Sometimes she went all the way out to the ranch.''

''She told you she drove out to the ranch in the middle of the night, and you believed her?''

''Of course I believed her. She was my wife. Sometimes I'd go out there the next day to join her.''

Jamie got a picture of a spoiled woman, running off to the boonies to get attention from her husband, making him run after her. She released a huge pent-up breath. ''Okay. I think I understand.'' She was letting her own frustration with this apparently immature woman get in her way. She had to get the conversation back on track. ''What made you finally call the police this time?''

''The fact that her car was still here…all of it.''

''All of it?''

''There were two wineglasses, used, sitting on the kitchen counter.''

''Yes. I remember. The police dusted them for fingerprints.''

Nathan nodded. ''But they only found Susie's prints—matching the ones on a perfume bottle I gave them. I figured she'd rinsed the glasses. She was very meticulous about our possessions.''

"And now the cops have stopped believing your version of things, anyway."

"Right."

"Tell me about that night again. Start from the beginning this time."

"I came home from the office late, intending to check in only long enough to pack so I could drive up to Kansas City that night. I had a big business meeting there the next day, and I was frustrated because I couldn't get a flight in time for that eight-o'clock meeting. So I decided to drive."

"And?" Jamie encouraged.

"And when I got home, Susie was all excited. She'd done a home pregnancy test. Positive. I couldn't believe it. Neither one of us could. We were dancing around the room, jumping up and down. We talked for quite a while, but then I went upstairs to pack."

"What time was that?"

"I don't know. Nine or ten. I figured we were all talked out and Susie would want to go to bed, anyway, and I could still drive all night and make my meeting. I was so stupid. She followed me upstairs, still talking excitedly. I'll never forget her face when she saw me pull my garment bag down. All she wanted was for me to stay in town so we could celebrate this long-awaited pregnancy. She begged me to stay. Why couldn't I just give her that?'' He braced an arm against the fireplace mantel and hung his head.

Jamie wanted to go to him, to touch him, to comfort him, but she was afraid. Afraid he might shrug off her touch, preferring to cling to his guilt, his memories, instead.

''Nathan,'' she said quietly, ''try to tell me the rest. It's important. Sometimes, not as often as I'd like, but sometimes, I pick up on little things that other people miss.''

He looked over his shoulder. A desperate look, to be sure, but she could tell he wanted to believe that she could help him. ''Things escalated into a fight. There's a balcony off the bedroom, and Susie marched out there. I followed her. I think that's what Mrs. Petree saw—our argument out there.''

''What did you argue about?''

''Everything. Like we always did. Susie would cry and get herself all angry and upset and say that I was neglecting her, that I didn't love her. I would try to reassure her, to tell her that I was only doing my job like a regular guy. But the truth was, I loved making money. Maybe on some level I was hoping a baby would distract her, make her less needy. Susie was cute and sweet, but she was very dependent, and she manipulated me so much that at some point in our marriage I just got tired of giving in to her demands, I think. I don't know. Maybe I decided there was no pleasing her. Anyway, when she got like that, it only drove me farther away.''

Understandable, Jamie thought.

''I'd get stubborn, like I did that night. I *wanted* to drive to Kansas City. I *wanted* to get away from her. I tossed my stuff into the garment bag in a hurry and stomped down the stairs. Susie threw that plant over the banister then—''

''The smashed fern the police found?'' Jamie had seen the photographs, courtesy of Brad Alexander.

He nodded and faced her fully. ''She wasn't aiming at me. She never hit me with the stuff she threw. It was just her way of expressing her frustration.''

Some people might call it abuse, Jamie thought, but she only said, very gently, ''What happened next, Nathan?''

''I drove off. I have no idea what she did after I left. After I drove down the road a ways, I started feeling bad about the fight, like I always did. I tried to call her several times, but only got the answering machine.''

''The FBI took that tape.''

''Yes. It's timed. It'll be used as evidence. Unfortunately, I was using my cell phone, so the M.U.D.'s—the phone company's records—''

''I know what M.U.D.'s are.''

''Those records won't show a location, but I

called from Bartlesville and from the small town in Kansas where I turned around, I know that for sure.''

''But now the DA is saying you planted those calls to give yourself an alibi.''

''Yes.''

''I turned around about two hours down the road. So I was gone about four hours altogether. I think it was after two in the morning when I got home.''

''And you have no idea what Susie was doing all that time?''

''No. The last time I saw her—''

''Wait,'' Jamie held her breath. ''The wineglasses. She knew she was pregnant—a pregnancy she had wanted for a long long time and she drank wine? That doesn't add up. Did you tell the police she was pregnant?''

Nathan closed his eyes and turned back toward the fire. ''No.''

''No?'' Jamie let her incredulousness come through loud and clear. *''No?''*

''No, and I won't. I don't even know why I told you. You're the only person who knows besides me. That information is strictly off the record.'' He turned and looked at her, his eyes calm but determined.

''You didn't tell the police that's what you were arguing about?''

"We weren't arguing about the pregnancy. We were arguing about my going out of town again."

"Nathan," she scolded, "even so, this pregnancy could be really important!"

"In what way? It's my personal business. It was a long time ago. It had nothing to do with her death. And it would only give my in-laws something else to grieve about."

Jamie decided to drop the subject of the pregnancy for now. She tapped a finger against her lips, considering whether to open the next Pandora's box. "Do you think Brad Alexander knows about all this? I mean, that Susie would run off from time to time?"

"Why do you ask?"

"Something he said to me, something really odd."

"What's that?"

Jamie had to decide again, right then: did she believe this man was innocent or not? She did.

"One time he called her 'poor Susie.' Isn't that a weird way for a DA to talk about a murder victim? It sounded so...unprofessional, really."

Nathan reacted to that information by narrowing his eyes.

"You have a bad feeling about him, too?" Jamie said.

"Call it a suspicion."

"Yeah. Something about Alexander doesn't add up."

Nathan came around the massive coffee table and lowered himself beside her on the couch. He sat with elbows propped on knees spread wide, angled toward her in a pose of urgency. "Like what?"

"Like the fact that he comes to *me* every time there's a new development in this case. Normally we reporters have to go digging for our sources. At one time I even wondered if it had something to do with…" Jamie quickly lowered her eyelids. "Never mind."

"If it had something to do with what? Jamie—" his voice dropped "—this is important to me."

"Well, I wondered if he wasn't trying to…to get to know me or something. You know, socially."

His chin jutted and he reached out to pick up his brandy, "I imagine there are lots of men who'd like to get to know you socially, but I doubt that's his motive." He drained the brandy. "If he wanted that, he'd just hit on you."

"True." Jamie frowned into the fire and nibbled at a hangnail.

Nathan cocked an eyebrow at her and studied her pretty face while she looked at the fire, picking that nail. He knew she was worrying. Worrying about *his* case, worrying about *his* life. And for the first time in days, he smiled. He liked this woman. God, he really liked her. She cared about people, and she was smart and down-to-earth and very pretty. No. She was much more than pretty. She was…hell, he couldn't put a word on it, unless it was *sexy*. But Jamie Evans's beauty was far deeper than mere sexiness. She raised the thumbnail to her lips again. Very mobile lush *interesting* lips.

"Can I ask you something?" he said.

"Sure." She blinked at the fire while she continued to chew in concentration.

"Do you have a boyfriend?"

Jamie stopped chewing and swiveled her head to him. "Why do you want to know that?"

"I told you the night of the ball that I'm attracted to you."

Her eyes went wide and her beautiful mouth fell open.

"Is that so surprising?"

Her mouth worked for a second before she said, "Well, *yeah*," the way teenagers do, sarcastically.

"Why? I'm a man. You're a woman. We're both single. Or are you? That was my question. I'm assuming you're free—if old Hugh was just… What'd you call him? A convenience?"

Jamie looked away. "I'm single."

"You're not currently involved with someone?"

She shook her head. "But I have been," she

added, he thought, somewhat defensively. "I've been involved."

"Me, too," he said quietly.

Jamie studied his solemn expression and wanted to ask him how he felt about his deceased wife now. But she was afraid of the answer. And all the news footage she'd pieced together told her just about everything she wanted to know, anyway. He had been crazy about her and most likely still was.

"I was actually engaged." Some part of her wanted him to understand that she'd had heartaches in her life, too. Not as traumatic as his, certainly, but she wasn't some shallow ingenue—that was what she wanted him to understand. "But it was...he was...it was a halfhearted relationship. Convenient." She bit her tongue for using that word. "Conventional," she tried again, and waved her hand. "I can't explain it."

"You didn't love him?"

She sighed. "I think I *wanted* to be in love. We'd been a couple in college. We got back together, several times, in fact. Our relationship went back and forth. Back and forth. But then..."

"You didn't love him." A statement this time.

She looked in his eyes and shook her head slowly, admitting it openly for the first time.

"And there's been no one else since? And there's no one now?"

"Oh, I have *dates*—" she realized she sounded defensive again "—all the time—"

"I bet you do." He leaned closer, tilted his head sideways to see into her face, while his brandy-scented breath fanned her cheek and his dark eyes explored her mouth again.

The sheer size and power of him made her want to melt into the couch cushions, and Jamie knew if she did that, she'd be a goner. She wouldn't be able to stop this man once he put his hands on her, and she wasn't about to let herself get involved with a man in his predicament. Her promise to her sister echoed in her mind.

"Let's be honest." His voice was throaty, low, as he continued to study her mouth. "As I said, I'm attracted to you, and I have been from the moment I saw you out on that ridge. And my guess is—" his gaze came up to her eyes, locked there "—you feel the same about me."

"I've gotta go." Jamie stood abruptly.

He folded his hands between his knees and lowered his head. "I'm sorry."

"Don't worry about it. I've just gotta go." Jamie felt like a heel as she turned to get her purse and the camera. The man had reached out to her. For him, that must have been hard. Why was she running away? But her conversation with her sister played across her mind again.

She got the camera strap adjusted and turned toward him.

He looked up and gave her face a questioning perusal. "What," he said, "are you so afraid of?"

"Nothing! I just can't afford to get involved with my subject. It's a…rule, a journalist's rule." She pushed her hair back and hefted her tote higher on her shoulder. "I can find my way out." She headed for the door.

He flipped on lights—chandelier, sidelights, overhead porch—as he followed close behind her. At the front door, he reached around her and grabbed the knob, but he didn't open it. "Your jacket," he said.

Jamie turned. "Oh, yeah."

He already had it in his other hand. "Here." He opened it to assist her.

"Thank you," Jamie let him slide the jacket over her arms. He held the lapels high, well above her shoulders. His hands never once touched her, even inadvertently, but somehow she still felt overwhelmed by his power.

"I understand," he said as he loomed over her, "if you don't want to get involved with me—with your subject, as you say. I'm not exactly…convenient, am I? I shouldn't have said anything. Maybe I've had a little too much to drink."

"It's okay. I just… It's my rule, that's all."

"You don't have to explain." He reached around and pulled an umbrella out of a stand. "May I walk you to your car?"

"No. I mean, I'm fine. But I'll borrow that if it's okay."

"Sure." He opened the umbrella for her.

Jamie took it, looked back at him once, and dashed out into the pouring rain.

Nathan closed the door and went inside to his empty house. He poured himself another finger of brandy and sat staring at the fire, wondering how his life had come to this.

All that time when he was married to Susie, when he was struggling to make her happy, trying to make their marriage work, he'd never once thought about another woman. What man, if he had landed a stunning wife like Susan Claremont, would think about another woman? But then, something had changed. Something had broken down. Sex for fun had become hollow. Sex as a chore became the rule.

The harder he tried to make Susie happy, the worse she seemed to feel. And somewhere in the back of his mind, he'd begun to wonder if he'd married the right woman, after all. But he'd tried to keep his life together, to keep *their* lives together despite his doubts. He'd pinned so many hopes on having that baby. He'd thought that with a baby they'd finally be happy, like Hunter and

Andrea. With a baby, Susie would feel fulfilled. But instead, Susie had disappeared, and that night his life had broken apart like shattered glass.

And now, *now,* when his world was completely in ashes, when he was headed for prison, appeals, maybe even the death penalty, for God's sake, he'd met Jamie Evans.

Jamie Evans. Honest and courageous. Endearing, with her messy hair and her chewed nails. Incredibly sexy.

But she was afraid of him—he'd seen it in her eyes. Women like Jamie Evans dated, got involved with and eventually married nice guys. Guys like he used to be. Guys who pulled in decent salaries doing something respectable. Guys who drove Suburbans around town, picking up the dry cleaning when they were told to. Not some wounded animal who sequestered himself on a remote ranch and had weird Indian visions while he hunted down some elusive killer.

And now he'd blown it by asking her if she was involved with someone. Why had he asked that? It wasn't as if they were going to go take in a movie and share a burger. What sort of relationship could he possibly offer her? And sex? Where? Her place? His place? He looked around the dark office, glowing with firelight and candlelight like some strange gothic cell. And him in it, the tragic hero. *Shit.*

He drained the brandy, and instead of feeling

some relief that at least he had these yearnings for a woman again, he felt more bereft than ever, realizing that at last he'd found someone he could truly love but couldn't have her. No, he could never have her.

BEFORE SHE EVEN GOT to the edge of the Biddle property, Jamie started wrestling with second thoughts. She had lied. There *was* no such rule. And she *was* afraid. Very afraid. But she wasn't afraid of the future with him, the way he thought. She was afraid of the past. Afraid he'd never get over it—over Susie.

By the time she'd walked to the corner, she wanted to turn around. She stopped and looked back at the mansion from under the dripping umbrella and somewhere in her mind faint strains of "On the Street Where You Live" echoed. His house was dark except for the foyer and porch lights he'd turned on as he'd followed her to the door. In the one-story wing, the bare arched windows above the draped corner windows glowed dull yellow from the firelight. She imagined him in that study, closed up with his old papers, his heart breaking all over again.

The unthinkable had happened to Nathan Biddle. Someone had murdered the woman he loved. And in his pain and his loneliness he'd reached out to Jamie. And she'd run from him, when what she'd really wanted to do was fling herself at him, touch him, kiss him. Suddenly Jamie didn't care what her sister thought; she didn't care about her boss's misgivings. All she cared about was Nathan Biddle. She turned around.

Thunder boomed as he opened the door. Jamie shivered under the umbrella. "I lied," she said simply.

He nodded while his eyes studied her face and the rain drummed on the narrow porch roof. "So. What *are* you afraid of? That I'm guilty?"

"No!" She shivered again. "I know that can't be true."

"How do you know?"

"I..." She looked up into his dark eyes. There was something strong and kind and reliable in their depths. The man she had come to know could never kill another human being.

"I just know. We will find the killer, Nathan. You've got to believe that."

He nodded. "So, what *are* you afraid of?" he repeated.

"I..." She was going to have force herself to say the words, but she knew this had better be said, and it had better be said *before* she got involved with him, *before* she fell in love with him. But hell, she was already falling in love with him, wasn't she? "I..." She started again. "I'm afraid you'll never get over your wife."

"I won't."

His honesty didn't make it any easier to accept that another woman would always be there, a woman he would never forget. Jamie actually felt her heart hurting. She'd never realized that the term "heartache" referred to a real physical sensation.

"But she has nothing to do with the way I feel about you."

Jamie took a moment to let what he had said sink in. It was true. The two them felt the way they felt about each other. Susie had nothing to do with that. Susie was in the past, and if Nathan could accept that, why couldn't she? "And how do you feel about me?"

He looked at her a long time. "I can't say."

"Because you don't know?"

"No. Because I can't put it into words. I've never felt this way before. I wasn't expecting to feel this way. I wasn't expecting *you*. I've been so lonely for so long, and suddenly I'm not lonely anymore because—" he spread a hand over his chest "—because now my mind is full of you."

Jamie drew in a sharp breath and held it.

"It's like—" he made a slow circle over his heart "—you're already part of me."

Jamie released her breath in one short disbelieving rush. He had just described how *she* felt about *him.* These past few weeks she hadn't been able to get him out of her mind.

"Now what?" she whispered when he didn't say anything more. Another shiver passed through her, but still he didn't move, didn't ask her to come inside.

"Now?" he said, and his voice was hoarse. "Now, before either of us takes another step, I think you need to understand something. I'm not convenient. With me, there will be no halfhearted relationship, no going back and forth."

For one long excruciating moment, they stood there, looking at each other, saying things with their eyes that mere words could never say. When Jamie finally nodded in understanding, he reached around the doorjamb and with one stroke of his big hand, flipped off all the lights. He stepped onto the porch, and in the distance lightning flashed, illuminating his intense burning eyes, his full mouth.

He took the camera and set it behind him, then slid her tote off her shoulder. He grabbed her wrist and pushed the umbrella back, keeping his eyes locked on hers. Jamie could feel the force of his dark gaze, penetrating every inch of her. Part of her wanted to back away from him, but she couldn't. She bit her lip, opened her fingers and let the umbrella bounce onto the concrete. He pushed her wet hair back, tilted her face up and framed her jaw with one hand. With his other arm he pulled her to him, bringing his strong body flush against hers. He was already hard.

Jamie mouthed, "Oh, God," as the thunder rolled over them and a fresh wave of shivers coursed through her body.

"With us," he whispered just before their mouths met, "there will be no going back."

CHAPTER NINE

EVERYTHING CHANGED in that one instant.

In that one instant the man Jamie had sworn not to get involved with became her lover, and she knew he was right. There would be no going back.

Their union was now a foregone conclusion, only a matter of time and place, a matter of how and where and when.

When the kiss ended she opened her eyes and looked up into his. His eyes were dark, solemn, but she could read no torment, no pain, in their depths. She saw only a promise—already silently given—of devotion. She saw his soul, laid open for her in that rainy darkness. "Jamie," he said hoarsely, "I can't believe this is happening."

"I can't either."

"But it *is* happening." His brandy-tinged breath warmed her lips as he spoke. "I've wanted to touch you like this from the first moment I saw you." His hands framed her rib cage and slid up, compressing her chest, gently, firmly, as if restraining a passion that might crush her. His thumbs circled up impatiently, barely caressing the undersides of her breasts. "It's like…like I said, I haven't been able to get you out of my mind from the very first. When I saw you fall into that flooding creek, my heart stopped. Even then, I think, on some unconscious level, I knew I couldn't let anything happen to you. I needed you, wanted you."

She kissed his jaw and was amazed that the intimate gesture already felt so right, so natural. His skin tasted warm, fresh, masculine, *real,* exactly the way she'd known he would taste. And she filled her senses with it.

"Every time I'm with you, it's all I can do to keep my hands off you," he confessed.

His thumbs kept up their insistent pressure, and Jamie longed to feel them directly over her nipples. She arched her back. "If only you knew how badly I've wanted this, too," she groaned. "But I've been trying so hard not to feel this way," she admitted.

"Me, too. For your sake. You have no business—" he brought his palm up to her temple and stroked her wild damp hair back "—getting involved with me. But, God, I'm so glad I feel this way at last. I'm so glad you're letting me touch you at last." He kissed her forehead tenderly. Then his arms squeezed her again as if driven by a force outside his control, as if he could not hold her tightly enough. And then he fastened his hot mouth to hers with that same force, as if he could not taste her enough.

This kiss was longer, hungrier. His hands flattened on her and she tilted her head as his mouth worked its amazing magic. Jamie felt the pull of that mouth from breast to belly and back. Oh, God. What was it going to be like with him?

He stopped kissing her and gave her a faint smile. "How does the song go? Something about not standing in the rain with me, or people might think we're in love? Let's go inside."

"No." Jamie suddenly regained her senses and pulled away. "I can't do this."

"Can't do what?"

"I can't stay here with you. I—"

"You mean in this house?"

Jamie nodded.

"Is it because of her?"

Jamie nodded again, whispered, "I'm sorry."

"Don't be sorry. We have to be completely honest with each other. The last thing I want to do is make you uncomfortable." He raised his head and looked up and down the rainy dimly lit street, which gave her another opportunity to study his perfect masculine throat, exposed above the open collar of the white shirt. Another chance to want him. "But let's go inside to talk about this. Nothing will happen, I promise." Like a gentleman, he calmly picked up her things, the umbrella, held the door open for her.

But when they stepped into the dark foyer, Nathan slammed the door, dropped the stuff and immediately clasped her slender body to his. He knew he had to restrain himself—she had legitimate misgivings—but he couldn't help himself. He was so...overjoyed to have her slender frame, her breasts, pressed fully against him at last.

"Just let me hold you," he whispered. After a moment he said, "I understand how you feel," against her hair. "I've felt the same way in this house myself. Like I couldn't breathe here. It's not a happy place, after all. And this isn't how I wanted our beginning to be. I wanted to wait until everything—the trial and all—was over. I'm sorry I came on to you like that. I don't know what got into me."

"Brandy," she said against his shirt.

He smiled.

"It doesn't matter how it happened." She laid her cheek against his shirt. "I don't want you to apologize for your feelings. And I don't want to wait." He heard her swallow. "We could go to my place."

Jamie waited for his response and felt a flood of relief when he finally nodded against her hair.

"We can go anywhere you say," he whispered. He tilted her face up and pressed his mouth to hers again, and again, his taste and scent filled her senses.

Then his head jerked up, and his body stiffened.

Jamie started to speak, but he pressed his fingers over her lips. "Listen," he whispered.

The sound of a key rattling in the lock made Jamie jump. He tightened his arms, kissed her temple. "It's okay."

He pulled the door open and a stunned-looking Robert stood on the dark dripping porch with a set of keys poised. "I forgot the alarm code and I think I got the wrong key. Hi, Jamie."

Nathan released Jamie and she tried to straighten her jacket. For a moment the whole thing felt like an awkward scene in some B movie. "Hi, Robert."

"Well," Nathan said, as Robert stepped into the foyer, "I take it this means you didn't have much luck in Pawhuska." He stepped behind Jamie and placed his hands lightly on her shoulders.

Robert registered one second of surprise at that gesture, then looked down at his high-top sneakers. "Nope. I went to the nursing home and the old man's granddaughter was there to give him a shave. She hardly let me ask him anything before she started in with that 'Grandfather is growing tired' bit." He looked at Jamie, explaining, "Some of those Osage women are overprotective of their elders." He looked back up at Nathan. "And sure enough, the old guy fell asleep before she even finished shaving him.''

''So you didn't get to ask him anything?''

Robert shrugged. ''Some. But once he was asleep, I left. When the horse is dead, dismount.''

''Who is this old man?'' Jamie looked over her shoulder at Nathan.

Nathan dropped his hands, and instantly Jamie missed the weight, the warmth. How could she have become so acclimated to a man's touch in such a short time? Because he had touched her in the right way, that's how. In exactly the ways she'd always dreamed of being touched. She would have smiled with giddiness at that realization, but Robert was looking on.

''I didn't tell you everything Frank found out,'' Nathan said. ''He picked up on a lead the cops missed. The bait shop guy got to shooting the breeze with Frank and suddenly remembered that there were two old men who always played dominoes in his store at the crack of dawn. The owner gave them free coffee and doughnuts. He thinks the old men were in there the morning he rented the nervous dude the canoe.''

''And Robert located these old men?''

''One of them has already died, but the store owner told Frank he thought one was in a nursing home up in Pawhuska. Frank found out the old guy is full-blood Osage, from a big close-knit family, so we thought it might be better if Robert went up there to talk to him first. He understands their ways.''

"But I struck out. Sorry, Nathan.''

Nathan assessed Robert's wet jacket and soaked sneakers.

"Let's get you dried off and go have something hot to drink while you tell me what you did find out.''

The three of them ended up in the mansion's surprisingly cozy kitchen. The ambiance of the room—soft task lighting, old wood cabinets, a gleaming black-and-white tile floor, aging white enamel appliances—made Jamie relax, although every time Nathan's eyes met hers she felt a certain undeniable tension. But with the rain softly pattering outside, even Robert's messiness seemed predictable and comforting. Robert stripped off his wet sweatshirt and pulled on a dry one, then dumped his wet shoes and socks in the corner while Nathan fixed instant hot chocolate. They seated themselves at a round oak table set into a bay window that overlooked the dark rainy backyard.

"The old guy—his name is Mr. Prettywater—'' Robert began ''—he is ninety-three, but he's still very sharp. You know why?''

"Why?'' Nathan said.

"Because he definitely remembers some strange

dude coming in to rent a boat at the bait shop. You know why?''

Nathan and Jamie sipped chocolate and waited.

"Because he knocked their dominoes table over.''

"Hmm.'' Nathan nodded.

"And he remembers that it was definitely about three years ago. You know why?''

Jamie rolled her eyes. For a highly educated man, Robert could certainly be a simple soul at times.

"Why?'' Nathan obliged, and raised his mug to his lips.

"Because he moved to the nursing home right after it happened, and he definitely remembers that. The granddaughter told me that was three years ago. The old man hates the place. Seemed like he was about to tell me more when the granddaughter took over and started shaving him. After that she did all the talking. She didn't want the old guy complaining to a stranger about living in the home, if you ask me. She said he had a big doctor's appointment the next day—lots of tests—and ran me off.''

"Then we'll have to go back,'' Jamie urged.

"I want to see him again, anyway,'' Robert's voice was enthusiastic. "I was wondering if the old guy knows any of the ancient poems. You never know with those fullbloods. There are only about twenty of them left.''

"There are only twenty Osages left? That's amazing!" Jamie was really surprised, and saddened, by that.

"Twenty *fullbloods*. We're all Osages," Nathan said. "Not just the fullbloods."

His cousin gave him a satisfied smile.

"Okay," Nathan said decisively. "We'll go back to Pawhuska day after tomorrow, before the old man forgets who we are."

"I agree," Jamie said. "Anything he has to say could be useful. There's got to be a way to find out who was wearing your jacket that day." Jamie took a notepad and pen out of her tote. She started to draw. "Here's a map to my complex. Third town house on the right."

Nathan took the map. "I know where this is. We'll pick you up first thing Wednesday morning, say, about six."

Jamie and Robert groaned and drained their mugs.

"Well, good night, Jamie." Robert got up and took the mugs to the sink, taking his time rinsing them. Jamie thought that most uncharacteristic, then realized he was giving them some privacy.

"I'll walk you to the car," Nathan said.

They gathered her equipment, and outside, under

the umbrella, he kissed her again. Mouths only, nothing else touching.

"Don't worry about Robert," Nathan whispered. "He's very…secretive by nature. He won't tell anyone."

She drew a huge breath. "I know." She exhaled. "When can we be together?"

"I don't know. I have to work—"

He pressed his lips to hers again. "Soon."

"Very soon," she promised.

THE MINUTE NATHAN WAS BACK, Robert said, "Was that what I think it was?" He grinned at Nathan.

"Yeah, it was exactly what you think it was— none of your business."

"Okay, wise guy. So do you like her?"

"Let's get some shut-eye."

"Well, *I* like her," Robert said. "Oh, not in the way you do, of course." He started up the stairs, but noticed Nathan turning to go into his study. "Aren't you turning in, Nathan?"

"No. I've still got some papers to look through in here."

"What papers? That old stuff I gave you the other night? Don't make yourself crazy looking at those, cousin."

"No stone unturned."

Robert sighed as Nathan closed the door. It was

a good thing Jamie Evans was a hell of a woman because it was gonna take a hell of woman to heal his cousin's soul.

NATHAN CROSSED THE ROOM and blew out the three pillar candles, which by now had burned low. Only the flames of the fire remained. He needed to turn on a lamp and read through all the notes, even if reading them made him heartsick.

Susie was involved with someone else. But what he'd read of the notes so far indicated it had been a one-sided relationship—this poor guy had been embarrassingly gaga about Susie, but she'd merely tolerated him—and that was some consolation. And it had been long ago. A high-school crush. That was some consolation, also. Still, it hurt that she'd never once mentioned the relationship in their many years of marriage.

He didn't want to think about any of it anymore. He didn't want the grief and the pain and disappointment. Right now he wanted to think about Jamie Evans. But how could he offer Jamie any kind of life together until this whole mess was straightened out? He went back to the notes. Suddenly he was so tired he could hardly keep his eyes open.

He sank onto the leather couch and stared at the dying flames. His eyelids felt heavy. His breathing and the rhythm of the dancing fire seemed to become one. As he breathed and watched the flickering orange and red, he let his weary eyes drift closed. The next thing he knew the flames leaped to life behind the veil of his eyelids. He was not sleeping, he was certain, yet he couldn't open his eyes. The fire shot higher, hotter. He rolled his head from side to side, heard the crackle of leather under him, but still, he could not open his eyes. From the flames a moon—or was it a sun?—rose like a shimmering ball, hot and cold at once, white as molten silver, standing above the flames like a sign, as if speaking to him. It seemed his vision stayed fixed on that moon for endless seconds, when suddenly from the edges of his vision, across the screen of his eyelids, a shadowy hawk circled and landed, spread-winged on the face of the moon.

He jerked up and his eyes flew open, only to see the same weak flames that had been there before. He put a hand to his forehead and felt beads of sweat there. An enormous headache pressed behind his eyes. He couldn't read the notes tonight. His mind—and his heart—had withstood enough for one day.

CHAPTER TEN

THE DREAM BOTHERED Nathan so much that he broke down and mentioned it to Robert the next morning. And immediately wished he hadn't.

They were watching another one of an endless string of movie comedies. Robert had a theory that watching these was therapeutic for Nathan.

But when Nathan said, "I had a strange…dream," Robert grabbed the remote and muted the tape.

"You mean another vision?"

Nathan shrugged. "Whatever."

"I'm telling you, Nathan, your Osage blood is in ascendance."

"Stop it."

"You stop it. You can deny your gift until your dying day, cousin, but you can't change it. What did you see?"

Against his better judgment, Nathan told him.

"Fascinating. Do you know what a hawk on the moon means?"

Nathan stared at the TV screen. Silently Goldie Hawn was acting up. He had no idea what a hawk on the moon meant, but he sure as hell wished there was some other explanation for these... dreams. "It means I'm losing my mind?" he finally said.

"No. Well, truthfully, it's hard to know what it means since you did not go looking for it—you didn't go on a quest. But it could mean that the spirits are trying to lead you to Susie's killer, since that is your quest now, your whole purpose."

"Then why don't the spirits just phone me up or send me an e-mail or something?"

"Or—" Robert ignored Nathan's sarcasm and stood up to pace "—it might even mean that the spirit of Susie herself is calling out."

Nathan's good-natured smirk vanished. "I'd appreciate it if you wouldn't talk about Susie and this Indian voodoo stuff in the same sentence."

"It's not voodoo." Robert leaned forward and snatched a copy of the *Tulsa World* off the coffee table. "And even if it is, who are you to be so skeptical? You are in trouble, cousin. You need protection. Look at this." He slapped his fingers on a front-page article, detailing the final results of Susie's autopsy. "Every time he gets half a chance, Van Horn is out on the stump, promising a conviction. There are always *new* developments in your case."

"Jamie's doing her best to see that my version of things gets equal time."

"Good for her. How long do you think that's going to last if her boss figures out you two are…getting close."

"That is none of your business, cousin."

"Hey, I know it isn't. But for the record, I was happy to see you with Jamie. I think it's high time you stopped living like a monk, and I told you, I think Jamie's really something. All I'm saying is, you've got to do everything you can to save yourself, and that includes going to see Elder Elliott. You need guidance."

"Now he's Elder Elliott?"

"Some of us like to call him that." Robert sounded defensive. "Some just call him plain old Lester. Whatever you call him, he's an Osage shaman. Aren't many left, my man. And you're lucky. This one's just up the road in Bartlesville." He dug between the couch cushions for a phone. "I'm calling him right now."

ON THE HOUR-LONG DRIVE north to the comfortable cultured oil-rich town of Bartlesville, Nathan began to feel uneasy. It was a gray day, cloudy. Rain, maybe even an early snow was gathering on the horizon. Why had he let Robert talk him into this nonsense? He felt even stranger as Robert steered the Mercedes down the broad avenue that led to the Phillips Petroleum complex at the heart of town. Nathan had been to these offices before, but on business, not for... what the hell were they here for? Indulging Robert's spookiness was the only answer Nathan could think of.

The skyscraper and surrounding buildings seemed incongruously tall and urbane, dominating the modest skyline of the town, which was tucked in the rolling green hills in the northeastern corner of Oklahoma. But this was where the massive Phillips empire had put down roots because this was where black gold lay beneath the earth. Robert pulled the Mercedes up to a parking meter.

"Elder Elliott is a retired executive of Phillips," he explained as he locked up the car, "and they still give him use of an office. We are meeting here at his request. Your coming and going from the Phillips building will be less suspicious than if we'd gone to his home out in the Osage Hills."

"Whatever." Nathan was disgruntled, more at himself than at his cousin. He searched his memory, trying to recall if he'd ever met Lester Elliott in person. He'd heard of the man in the course of business, and Mr. Elliott was well respected—but a shaman? He hoped this meeting wasn't going to turn into some huge embarrassment for both of them. As an elevator whisked him and Robert to the eighteenth floor, he ruminated about what a stupid *desperate* little excursion this was, considering his overwhelming problems. *A shaman.*

A long hallway led to the open door of a quiet

impersonal office. Walnut paneling. Tasteful art. Broad windows revealing a view of the Osage Hills, far to the west. A white-haired gentleman in a nondescript gray suit turned from the windows to greet them. His placid expression and drooping features reminded Nathan of a gentle old hound dog. His bearing radiated dignity, and the deep crescents framing his mouth might have been rakish dimples in his youth.

Robert stepped forward on light feet and respectfully handed the man something wrapped in plain white paper. Nathan hadn't noticed the small package before, but if he knew Robert, it contained tobacco or some other traditional gift for a shaman.

The old man nodded and took it without comment. Then, with no introduction or preamble, he said to Robert, "Is he sensitive?"

"No." Robert replied, then leaned confidentially toward Nathan. "Sensitive means that you can see the future," he whispered, "or tell what a man is thinking—stuff like that."

Nathan gave his cousin a dry look, thinking he could certainly tell what Robert was thinking, and it was mostly bullshit. But he had to admit the old man was a surprise. He didn't look like the character Nathan had envisioned. His eyes, rheumy, dark and deep-set, patiently studied Nathan from under those drooping lids.

"Come in here and sit."

They lowered themselves, three large Osage men, into plush leather chairs, and as they arranged their long legs, Nathan had a sudden notion that they could just as easily be situating themselves around a campfire, instead of a glass-topped table with a model of an oil-fractionating plant in the center of it. Robert and the old man shared a quiet, gentle, almost stoic quality. Nathan, with his aggressive energy, felt a bit like an outsider.

The old man started in right away. "You must be careful now," he said. "For you are traveling two worlds with one spirit."

Nathan frowned and gave his cousin a sidelong glance. "I don't know about that, Mr. Elliott. All I know is my cousin insists that you have certain...abilities. As for myself, I don't know about any of this. I wasn't all that close to my mother's family. I never paid much attention to Osage ways. And now that I've got trouble, I'm not about to turn into some instant Indian, looking for easy answers."

"I will not give you any answers, easy or otherwise, because you already have all the answers you need. In here." He touched his crisp white shirtfront. "And it is what is in here—" he tapped his breastbone harder "—that makes one Indian...or not. If what your cousin has told me is true, you have the heart of the Osage, whether you want to have it or not."

If you were any kind of shaman at all, Nathan wanted to say, *you'd be able to see that my heart is like stone.* "What, exactly—" Nathan couldn't help the sarcastic spin he put on the words "—has my cousin told you?"

As he typically did in these situations, Robert sat as silently as a boulder.

"He said when you were younger, you lived as the whites do, chasing after money. But when your wife disappeared, you retreated to the Hart Ranch out in those hills—" he raised an arm toward the massive windows "—and out there, he believes you found your spirit. That is because the Hart Ranch is a special place. It is no accident that old Black Wing chose to live up there on that ridge, near the Weeping Faces."

Nathan opened his mouth in a question, but Lester droned on, "It is no accident that he took Rose, daughter of a great medicine bundle priest, as his second wife. This is the blood you have come from. Now, your cousin says, you have come to Tulsa and put the white man's suits on again, but only so that you can find your wife's killer."

"Mr. Elliott, you seem to forget that I'm part Biddle, too. Maybe I intend to go back to my life in Tulsa permanently when this is all over. I like Tulsa. I *liked* making money. And I'm guessing you're part white, too, Mr. Elliott. This office—" he chopped a hand at their opulent surroundings

"—is no tepee. We are all twenty-first-century men, nothing like the ancients, not like Black Wing."

"No, you are not like the ancients. Unlike the ancients, you will always have to travel two worlds, but no matter what, you will always have the Osage blood in you. Times change, blood does not. And as for me, I am not long for this or any other century."

Nathan couldn't keep from rolling his eyes. This was the kind of talk he'd expected. Fancy office or not, this was just another dramatic old Indian, caught up in outdated mysticism.

But the old Indian merely blinked at Nathan's barely concealed impatience and continued. "You will never go back to your old life. You are like an eagle, raised among chickens. You no longer want to scratch the dirt after seeing the sky. And your heart, the heart of the Osage—" he tapped his chest again "—is not so hardened as you seem to think." He continued to tap his chest lightly, in a steady rhythm. "On the contrary. It is waiting— beating—for another."

Nathan stared at the old man's tapping fingers and felt something catch in his own chest. He hadn't said that part about his heart turning to stone out loud, had he? Frowning, he suppressed the un- comfortable feelings that the shaman's words had stirred up and glanced accusingly at Robert, who merely gave his long-suffering shrug.

As for the old man's prediction of "another," the image of Jamie Evans had come to mind, and against his will Nathan felt the familiar surge of hope and longing that he'd tried to resist in recent days. How could he have a relationship with Jamie when his wife's killer was still roaming the earth? It seemed disloyal, wrong. But the old man had guessed it—or had *seen* it. Nathan's heart was indeed now beating for another. And shaman or not, somehow the old man had also explained exactly how Nathan felt about living in Tulsa. How could he go back to that narrow, sterile life he had lived on Owasso Street with Susie? How could he go back to that stuffiness after breathing the free air of Hart Ranch? He had changed during his years of self-imposed exile, and there was no going back.

"So now you have these visions," Elliott said, breaking the protracted silence. "But your cousin tells me they are coming unbidden. This is not good. Without guidance you may attract something negative. So tell me what you have seen, and I will tell you what I think."

Robert gave Nathan a small encouraging nod.

Nathan sighed. What did he have to lose? In only a few months Trent Van Horn would stand before a jury and ask for the death penalty. He pinched the bridge of his nose as he started. "None of these…visions means anything to me. The first one happened the day Susie's body was discovered. Faces carved in the clouds—''

''Which way were you facing when you saw this image?'' the old man interrupted.

That was easy. The picture window in his grandfather's house, the sunset. Nathan felt a wave of nausea, remembering that sunset, how it transformed before his eyes. How he had felt so bereft, so lost all over again, the same way he had in the days immediately after Susie disappeared. ''West.''

The shaman nodded. ''West…for war.''

Nathan started to speak, but Robert poked him, giving a silent warning when Nathan frowned at him: *Do not question.*

So Nathan told about the giant willow tree— upside down—with the fronds draping to earth like thousands of golden violin strings.

And he told about the hawk on the moon.

The old man interrupted only one time to mutter, ''The willow tree is your family, I think, which must be restored.'' Other than that, he listened with his gaze fixed in the distance, toward those gentle green hills outside the tall windows.

''You must be careful,'' the old man finally repeated the same words he'd said when they first entered his office. Which irritated Nathan. *I must be careful? Really?* When he'd been accused of murder, when the case against him grew stronger every day, when the prima donna local DA was looking to make a coup before an election? His own use of an Indian phrase set his teeth on edge.

But something Jamie Evans had said kept him from dismissing the old man and all that he stood for outright. "Intuition," she had claimed, "is the strongest tool of an investigative reporter—and the hardest to come by." *Intuition.* If Jamie thought there was some value in it, maybe he'd consider it.

"Grandfather," Robert finally said, "please be more specific. Nathan may be put to death if we do not find the killer. What are the spirits trying to tell us?"

The old man had not looked at Robert since he had taken the white package. When he looked now, his sleepy eyes were suddenly focused, sharp. "You are having visions, too?"

Nathan had never seen his cousin blush. "Well, no," Robert stammered. "I only meant—"

"Then the spirits aren't trying to tell *you* anything."

"Sorry," Robert muttered.

The old man glanced at the package. "Because you have shown respect, I will ignore your impertinence." He fell silent and stared out the windows again. When at last he finally spoke the words came out in one long stream: "These visions do not come from the dead. They come from inside you, from your spirit helper, who does not want you to die. In the old days a young man went on a vision quest alone in the woods. In his isolation and deprivation, the spirits would take pity on him and come to assist him. While he was gone a shaman could send up smoke from the pipe to keep him safe. After such a young man completed his quest, dreams from the spirit helper might come for the rest of his life. I believe your time alone on your ranch was somehow like a vision quest. Because of this, you have changed.

"Now, in your desperate situation, your spirit helper has come to your aid. Therefore it is important to heed these visions. It is important to pay attention. Your mother's people were close to the elements, and so it is the elements that will guide you. The clouds, the trees, the water. Look to these. But especially look to the fire. Face east each morning and ask Grandfather Sun to dispel the darkness you feel. Ask him to guide your steps. Like the eagle, you have been flying alone. But in time you must become even more like the eagle, whose head, white like snow, represents purity. In time you will know the meaning of what you see. You will believe it. In here." He tapped his heart again and looked at Nathan. The old hound-dog eyes, as deep and dark as lost lakes, were so intense that Nathan looked away. "It will be like breathing,'' the shaman continued. ''Until then, wait for the snow to cover your path. After the snow melts, you can make new tracks, as you continue traveling two worlds.''

The old man fell silent again.

Nathan sat there, refusing to put too much stock into this shaman talk—Elliott could have gotten everything he'd said out of a book. The guy probably didn't know any more about the future than Robert's old dog.

When it was clear that nobody else was going to speak, Robert said, ''Thank you, Grandfather,'' very quietly.

Nathan shook his head and stood. ''Let's go. I appreciate your taking the time to see us, Mr. Elliott.''

The old man rose stiffly from the leather chair. He was tall, still powerfully built, pushing eighty at least and had probably been given a couple of elaborate retirement parties to prod him out of this building. But it still seemed as if he belonged in this office, *possessed* it. His style, his presence, permeated the place the way a bear imprinted a den. He turned to the windows. With his back to them, he said, ''Do not forget the fire.''

''That was most helpful,'' Nathan mumbled when the elevator doors had closed on them.

''I'll say.'' Robert was sincere.

"He didn't tell me anything I didn't already know."

"Oh, he didn't? All that stuff about Grandmother Rose and Black Wing—"

"People all over Osage County know stories about Hart Ranch. Maybe the old chief just wanted to combine the lands to make the ranch bigger. All that's a matter of record, tribal or otherwise. The fact is, Grandpa Biddle and Ruby Hart made the ranch the size it is today when they got married in 1916. Period. There's nothing magic about the land, and I didn't go on any vision quest out there."

Robert folded his arms in a pout and said nothing more about it until they were on the road back to Tulsa.

"I saw your face when he told you that you're falling in love with Jamie Evans. That's not a matter of public record."

Nathan squinted. "He didn't say anything about Jamie Evans."

Robert turned to his cousin, his eyebrows raised above his sunglasses. "I think she's falling for you, as well."

"Watch the road." Nathan wanted to keep his cousin's nosy mind off this delicate subject. "I have to admit, what he said about the fire got my attention."

"Because you saw the hawk in the fire?"

"No."

"What, then?"

"It got me thinking about that Tallgrass Prairie fire. The sheriff told Frank it had been ruled arson."

"Then you think the shaman was telling you to look for something besides visions when he said look to the fire?"

"Maybe."

Robert fell silent, thinking. "I keep wondering, who would want to burn up a bunch of Japanese grass out on the Tallgrass Prairie when the forest service does that several times a year, anyway?"

"Maybe that's not what they were trying to burn up."

Robert turned his head, frowned.

"Watch the road."

"We know we put Grandfather's knife back in his cabin after that blood-brothers business when we were kids, right?"

"You bet your ass we put it back. I was afraid the old man would tan our backsides with a piss-elm switch."

"So how'd it end up under a rock at the mansion?"

"Yeah. Weird."

"But we know it's been gone awhile. When you moved into the cabin so many years after Grandfather died—"

"I assumed it was still right where we stashed it, up on the mantel behind all that other junk."

"But when you set about cataloging his things—"

"It was missing. I thought that maybe one of the aunties had squirreled it away at her house. I figured it would show up sooner or later."

"It did."

"Yeah. Right after Grandfather's cabin burned. That doesn't make sense. If the knife was used on Susie and somebody was trying to destroy it... I am confused, cousin."

"Here's what we know. You and I know the knife was in the cabin at one time. Susie was slashed with a heavy knife across her collarbone."

"Grandfather's knife shows up at the Tulsa mansion."

"Planted there."

"With Susie's DNA, my DNA, your DNA..."

"And some unidentified person's DNA..."

"All in the dried blood under the hilt."

"Cynthia's going to have me tell that blood-brothers story on the stand, you know."

Nathan nodded. "I appreciate that. I know you don't want to talk about stuff like that in public."

"But it will show how your blood got under the hilt of that knife. Cynthia says we have to establish reasonable doubt about the unidentified blood on the knife. So you're thinking whoever planted the knife at the mansion is the same person who took it from the cabin and the same person who set the wildfire and—''

"The same person who killed Susie.''

Robert grew thoughtful. "The shaman wanted us to know that the fire was the key.'' His voice was awestruck.

"Maybe. But it's still a key with no lock. The question is, what was the arsonist trying to destroy with that fire, and how the hell do we ever find this person even after we figure that out?''

"I do not know, cousin, but there has to be a way.''

"Let's get some grub and head home. Tomorrow we've got a full day in the teaming metropolis of Pawhuska, Oklahoma.''

"Yeah. In the exciting company of Mr. Mason Prettywater and his granddaughter.'' Robert paused. "And the lovely Jamie Evans.''

CHAPTER ELEVEN

"PAWHUSKA, OKLAHOMA," Robert announced as Nathan steered his Mercedes off the old state highway 99 onto Main Street, "capital of the proud Osage Nation. Did you know that eighty-six of this small town's ninety-eight buildings are listed on the National Register of Historic Places?"

"Robert, cut the guided tour," Nathan said dryly. "Jamie doesn't want to hear it."

But Jamie did want to hear it. Nathan had grown up around here, had gone to high school here, and Jamie wanted to know as much as she could about this small town. She adjusted her sunglasses and peered to her right, glimpsing the Osage County Historical Museum as the Mercedes whizzed past. "Tell me more, Robert."

Robert unbuckled his seat belt and leaned forward, obviously excited about his subject. "We're coming up on the historic downtown. The old railroad depot will be on the left, then in short order, we'll pass the triangle building."

Jamie caught only a quick glimpse down

Kihekah Avenue toward the historic district. "Could we slow this tank down?"

"Uh-uh."

Nathan, she knew, wanted to get to Mr. Prettywater as early in the day as possible, before the old man got too tired to tell his story. They crossed Bird Creek, then Clear Creek and made a right turn onto Pecan Street where the Pawhuska Nursing Home waited in the sleepy well-tended way of small-town nursing homes everywhere.

The temperature had dropped thirty degrees since yesterday, as it often did this time of year in Oklahoma. Jamie looked up at the raw gray sky, pulled her thin sweater closer and dashed into the colonial brick building without waiting for Nathan and Robert to catch up.

When the men stepped through the door, the nurses recognized Robert and waved them past with a smile. The trio found Mr. Prettywater in his room, dozing in a wheelchair with a white institutional blanket wrapped around his bony legs.

"Mr. Prettywater?" Robert squatted down to the old man's eye level. "Remember me? Robert Hart? This is my cousin, Nathan."

"Hello, boys." Mr. Prettywater smiled and eyed both men. "Are we goin' to the I'n-Ion-Schaka?"

"No, sir," Robert said. "That's in June. It's November now."

"The annual Indian dances," Nathan whispered to Jamie.

"Oh," she said.

"Who is this pretty one?" The old man's eyes brightened as he indicated Jamie.

"This is Ms. Evans. She's a...a friend of Nathan's," Robert said.

"Hello, Mr. Prettywater." Jamie took his frail hand gently and held it for a second. "Thank you for seeing us."

"I think I seen you on TV." He nodded at her.

She crossed to the freshly made-up bed and perched on the edge so he could get a better look at her. "Yes. Channel Six." She smiled. "The boys told me you were sharp."

"Uh," Prettywater grunted. "Sometimes. Sometimes not so sharp. I am tired today. They took a buncha pictures of my gut yesterday. It's not so nice to be old sometimes."

"We won't keep you long, sir," Robert said. "Mr. Prettywater, do you remember when I came to see you a few days ago?"

Prettywater fixed his keen old eyes on Robert and gave one wobbly nod of his head.

"Do you remember what we were talking about? The rude young man who knocked over your domino game in the bait shop?"

Another nod. "My dadgum granddaughter cut it

short. Our talk, that is. Not the dominoes.'' He chuckled merrily at his little joke.

"Right.'' Robert chuckled, too, and nodded encouragingly.

"Dadgum woman won't let me be. Just like her mother. Real bossy.''

"Nathan and I really need to know more about what happened that morning at the Green Country Bait and Boat Shop,'' Robert urged.

"You were about to tell him something important,'' Nathan put in.

"I was?'' The old man seemed momentarily confused, but Nathan and Robert waited with breath-holding patience. Robert, balanced on the balls of his feet. Nathan, standing like a statue with his arms folded across his chest. Jamie wound her legs together like rope and chewed a nail.

"One ass,'' the old codger chuckled.

"Pardon me?'' Robert said.

"And I was winnin' the dadgum game!'' the old fellow suddenly exclaimed. "And that dadgum turkey knocked the dadgum table over!''

"And then what?'' Nathan stepped forward to encourage him.

"I'm tired today,'' the old man announced, his energy apparently depleted by his outburst.

"Mr. Hart. Here you are again.'' A very large woman with a tight silver-and-black topknot sailed into the room, tilting her head at Robert.

Jamie jumped up off the bed. Here was an intimidating creature if ever she saw one.

"Good morning, Grandfather." When the woman put her hands on the old man's shoulders and bent to kiss his head, thick hammered silver bracelets flashed at her wrists.

"Juanita," the old man flapped a hand. "I'm too tired for a shave today."

"That's fine, Grandfather." She patted his shoulder. "I'll comb your hair for you or something."

She rose to her full imposing height, and above her high cheekbones, her black eyes did not look happy. "I'm sorry. You must leave now. Grandfather is tired."

Robert stood up. "Same old song," he muttered to Nathan.

Nathan showed more tact. "We're sorry. We didn't mean to fatigue him. Would there be a better time?"

"There is no better time. I understand that you are in a perilous position, Mr. Hart. We get the news out here in Pawhuska, too." Her eyes flashed at Jamie. "But my grandfather has told you all he knows about the day his dominoes got knocked over. I won't allow him to be repeatedly questioned or dragged into Tulsa for some ghastly murder trial." She folded her arms over her chest as if to say she had spoken.

"Goodbye, Mr. Prettywater." Nathan squatted down in front of him. "I thank you for your time."

They drove to the Bluestem Café for some lunch.

"That woman can't stay there all day," Robert groused. "If we hang around, we can go back when her car's gone. She drives that big green Lincoln."

"What was he mumbling about 'one ass'?" Jamie mused.

"Seemed a little confused if you asked me." Robert shrugged.

"I wondered the same thing," Nathan said.

Before their chicken-fried steaks had arrived, snow flurries started twirling in the gray air outside the picture window. And by the time they headed back to the Mercedes, the snow had turned into sleet.

"Do you think it's going to get really nasty?" Robert said.

Nathan tugged on the brim of his hat. "Looks that way." He opened the car door for Jamie. "Maybe I'd better get Jamie back to Tulsa. She can't miss work."

"What about the old Indian?"

Nathan shook his head. "Guess we'll have to come back out."

When he climbed into the back seat of the Mercedes, Robert said, "Take me over to Billy's. I can borrow his truck. If the roads get bad, he keeps a set of chains for tires. You all go on back to Tulsa. I'll talk to the old man again. As soon as the lovely Juanita and her big green Lincoln are gone.''

Jamie craned her neck. ''Find out about the 'one ass' thing, okay?''

BUT EVEN BEFORE they reached the cutoff to the highway, the roads grew worse. ''When do you have to be back at work?'' Nathan asked.

''Not until tomorrow.''

The atmosphere in the Mercedes had turned intimate the moment Robert climbed out at Billy's auto-repair shop. They hadn't touched, but Jamie knew it was just a matter of time before they would. Now he was asking the kind of question where one thing led to another. ''Not until the afternoon, actually.''

''Then I'm going to suggest we head back down Highway 11 and go up to the ranch. That's a ten-mile trip versus fifty miles back into Tulsa. This 'tank,' as you called it, is trying to slide all over the place.''

Jamie had felt the Mercedes go into a gentle skid or two. She looked out the windshield; the wipers could hardly keep up with the pelting ice crystals. They'd already passed one unfortunate party whose car was in the ditch, and Nathan had used his cell phone to alert Robert and Billy to come to their aid.

"Unless you'd be more comfortable at the Black Gold Motel back in Pawhuska."

She smiled. "No thanks. I'll take my chances with you."

At the ranch house he pulled the Mercedes up close to the long porch and said, "Wait." He dashed around the car, pulling his jacket off as he went. "Here." He wrapped it around her shoulders.

Jamie had not been inside the large ranch house before. She was relieved to see that the decor was masculine and austere and had no hint of Susan Biddle's influence. Nathan went directly to the massive stone fireplace and got busy stacking kindling.

When the flames flickered up and caught, he turned to her. "Well, here we are."

"Yes." Jamie slipped his jacket off and laid it on the back of the big leather sectional sofa. She walked up to the fire and stood there hugging her sweater to herself, suddenly shy as a schoolgirl.

He, too, looked uncomfortable. "Are you hungry or anything?"

She gave a little laugh.

"Oh, yeah. We just finished off a famous Bluestem Café chicken-fried steak."

She nodded, placing a palm on her flat stomach. "I may never eat again!"

He smiled. "Yeah. Well. Let's have a seat."

She walked around the sectional and sat down, close to the edge.

He seated himself near her, but not within touching distance. He, too, sat on the edge with his knees spread wide, his elbows propped on them, his hands clasped. The timeless pose of a man with something on his mind.

Jamie, who could carry on an interview with a fence post, found she had nothing to ask, nothing to say. She made a heroic effort to sit calmly and not nibble her nails.

He maintained his tense pose until the large logs above the kindling burst into flame. Watching the fire, he reached across the space between them and took Jamie's hand. He rubbed his thumb in her palm, tenderly, repeatedly. It seemed an eternity went by while Jamie's heart pounded and her chest felt as if it might burst.

Finally he said, "Jamie, look at me."

When their eyes met, he whispered, "You realize, of course, that I already love you."

When she gave him the barest tiniest nod, he made one swift move across the space that separated them and put his hands on her—one around her shoulders and one splayed lightly over her heart. He looked into her eyes as he settled her against the thick pillows at her back. His gaze fell to her lips as he whispered what he'd said before. "No going back."

CHAPTER TWELVE

THE NEXT DAY, second thoughts assailed Jamie like a swarm of pesky gnats. Nathan's words, *No going back,* which had sounded so strong, so sure, when he'd murmured them, started to take on a slightly threatening ring to Jamie the minute she woke up and found herself in his ranch house...in his master bedroom...in his enormous four-poster bed. The room, unnaturally brightened by the fresh blanket of snow outside, seemed cold and unfamiliar. She remembered, of course, exactly how she'd gotten in the bed. He'd picked her up and carried her there. She turned to her side and pulled the heavy down comforter tighter over her bare shoulders.

No going back? She kept wondering what he meant by that.

She studied him as he slept peacefully beside her. He was a magnificent specimen of a man. But even more compelling than his good looks, he had been the most tender, the most thrilling lover she could ever have imagined. She burrowed down in the sheets and smiled at him. She had actually sensed that he'd be this way the first moment he'd touched her. But again his words came back to bedevil her and she frowned.

No going back? She'd seen enough of Nathan Biddle these past few weeks to know that when he spoke, he meant what he said. She couldn't possibly get involved in anything so permanent-sounding. Her station manager had been right. She'd gotten in over her head with this enigmatic man, and now the relationship was spinning out of control. And it had become sexual. Definitely. Suddenly Jamie wanted to pull the comforter over her head. She didn't even want to imagine what her sister would have to say about this turn of events.

She slid out of bed, shivering in the cold air. She passed up the Navajo blanket robe he'd offered her last night and dressed in her clothes.

Jamie padded to the bank of windows, overlooking the winding river and the Osage Hills. She studied the landscape and remembered every move, every sensation, every breath. She simply could not believe how incredible sex with Nathan had been. With Donald, she'd always hoped that the sex would improve with time. Maybe, she'd reasoned, all they needed was more confidence, more trust, more experience.

But now, that sort of thinking had gone out the window. If only she'd known! It really had nothing to do with confidence, trust or experience. It had to do with passion, an element that was clearly lacking in her first relationship and was clearly present in this one. From that first kiss, Nathan Biddle had made no secret of how badly he wanted her. And he'd practically taken her apart when they finally got into bed!

She glanced back at him one last time as she left the room. His body, completely relaxed in sleep, still exuded power. But this relationship was already about far more than sex, had been from the start. She admired him. And he admired her; she was pretty certain of that.

Still, there were all these...complications. On her way down the stairs she decided that they would definitely have to keep their involvement a secret until after the trial—that was the only sane way. Any hint of an affair would expose them both to horrendous gossip. Something neither of them could afford. She was making the turn on the landing, chewing a nail and ruminating worriedly, when she ran smack into Robert, standing at the bottom.

"Robert!" she yelped. For a big man, he certainly didn't make much noise when he moved about.

"Jamie!" he cried, also taken aback.

Then they both spoke at once.

"I didn't know you guys were here."

"I thought you stayed in Pawhuska last night."

"Uh, well, I did...but it's not night anymore. It's...uh, morning now." The big man was clearly embarrassed.

"Uh, yes, it is morning. I mean, the storm got worse and we couldn't make it back to Tulsa. So we stayed here. Nathan's upstairs." Jamie looked over her shoulder. "I don't think he expected you to come by here. How'd you get here?" Jamie, always able to control her voice, managed to keep it casual, calm, but inside she was screaming. So much for secrecy.

Even now, Robert was smiling at her with that sappy knowing look people adopted when they thought somebody else was falling in love. "My old friend Billy? He loaned me his truck. We put chains on the tires."

By George, Robert had better not breathe a word of this to another living soul. But Nathan had said Robert could keep a secret. *He'd better! Dammit!* Why, oh why, had she let Nathan Biddle get to her last night? It was his eyes...and his voice and his hands and his smell, and his...oh, it was all of him, just plain all of him.

All of him came thumping down the stairs in his robe and stocking feet at that precise moment. "Man! It's colder'n a cave in this house. Hey, cousin! When did you get here?"

"Just now."

"Uh, Jamie—" Nathan stopped beside her on

the landing ''—I hope your accommodations were comfortable, that you slept well. I apologize for forgetting to turn on the heat upstairs before we retired.''

He was smooth, she'd give him that. And none of it was a lie. Jamie relaxed. Of course. Robert would have no idea in which of the numerous upstairs bedrooms she'd slept.

''I was very warm and comfortable, thank you.'' She smiled sweetly at Nathan.

''Any luck with Mr. Prettywater, cousin?''

Robert shook his head. ''The granddaughter took him to the doctor again. I've gotta go back.''

''Okay, then. Anybody want a cup o' java?'' Nathan sprinted toward the kitchen.

''He's in a good mood,'' Robert observed in that flat-toned voice Indians employed when something else is implied.

''Yeah. Maybe it's the weather.'' She said it sarcastically because Robert's nosiness was getting on her nerves.

''Snow has that effect on some people,'' he replied.

In the enormous kitchen Nathan remained cheerful while he efficiently made coffee. The refrigerator was stocked, Robert's doing, Jamie supposed, and while they munched on fresh fruit and doughnuts, they made plans.

Nathan would drive Jamie back into Tulsa in his

four-wheel drive Durango so that she'd make it to work on time. Robert would stay at the ranch and tend the horses. Nathan would return to the ranch and then he and Robert would go back into Pawhuska to return the truck and visit the old man one more time, trying to catch him after his nap, when he might be less fatigued and when his bossy granddaughter wouldn't interrupt.

The drive to Tulsa, even though the storm had stopped, was still slow. The lesser roads were snow-covered and the county bridges icy.

Jamie, anxious to get to her town house and a nice hot shower, was disappointed when they turned off the interstate in Tulsa and Nathan wanted to swing by the Owasso street house first.

"I'd take you straight home—" he picked up on her reaction "—but I want to show you something I found the other night." He reached over and squeezed her hand, and Jamie returned the affection.

"I want you to know something, Nathan."

"Okay." He continued to stroke her palm with his thumb.

"I...I've only been involved with one other man. And it...it sure wasn't like this."

"Oh? Is that a good thing or a bad thing?"

She wanted to punch his shoulder, but he was driving. "How can you even ask such a question after last night?"

He raised her hand to his mouth and pressed his warm full lips to her fingers. He kept his eyes on the road. "Jamie," he said huskily, still clutching her hand, "as long as we're making confessions here, I've gotta tell you, it's never been like this for me, either. You've made me feel alive again. I wanted you the minute I woke up. I gotta tell you, I was not happy to see you already dressed and old Robert standing at the bottom of the stairs."

"I wanted you, too."

"Then why weren't you in my bed when I woke up?"

Jamie looked down at their laced fingers. "I got up and got dressed because…I guess because I'm still scared."

"Scared? Of me?"

"No! I mean, yes, in a way. I'm scared of the kind of man you are."

"Jamie, I wish you'd known me before all this happened in my life."

"That's not what I mean. I'm not afraid of your past. I understand what you've been through. I'm scared of the way you don't hold back. I'm scared of how you're not afraid of anything, of anyone, not even of your own feelings. I'm scared of how you don't do things casually."

"By 'things' do you mean making love?"

She blushed and nodded.

He grinned. "That's the last thing I'd ever hold back."

"That's what I'm talking about. And I love that about you, but it scares me, too. And what you said was, no *going* back, not holding back."

"There's a difference?" he said softly.

"Yes. No going back—that sounds like we're talking about the future. Or did you just mean, no going back...sexually?"

"I meant no going back in my heart. Jamie, I don't think two people can get involved with each other, sexually and emotionally, and then go their merry way as if nothing happened."

She studied his profile, then looked down at his body. He was still holding her hand against his thigh, driving with one hand on the wheel. His arms were powerful, his shoulders broad, his legs bulked with muscle. He was bright and kind, honest and caring. And he'd just told her in so many words that he wasn't afraid of commitment. What the devil was wrong with her? "Maybe it's just me. Maybe I'm just a spoiled city girl who can't handle a down-to-earth guy like you."

"Down-to-earth?"

"Not down-to-earth, exactly. More like a guy with nothing to lose."

"I wouldn't say I've got nothing to lose. I've got you."

"That's just it, Nathan. Look at you. You're already in love."

"Yes, I am."

"I think I am, too, and it scares the pee out of me. I guess I'm afraid of what a commitment to you might require of me."

"Like what?"

"Like giving up pieces of myself. I told you, I'm a reporter. That's what I do. I'm a city girl. Last night out on that lonely ranch... Aren't you even a little bit worried about how this will all turn out?"

He kissed her hand again. "Seems a little early for that. First we have to do everything in our power to catch the killer. That's the most crucial step to making it all turn out okay—for us."

And when had this shift in his thinking happened? she wondered. Suddenly his motivation for catching the killer had shifted from his past to his future...his future with Jamie. Surely this was true love, she thought. Surely this was the kind of miraculous change true love could bring.

When they got to his mansion, he took her to the office, straight to the mahogany desk in the corner. "Tell me what you know about Brad Alexander." He opened a drawer and drew out some folded papers.

"You mean, have I done a background check

on him? Not really. He's...he's not the suspect here, Nathan.''

"Maybe he should be. It just so happens," he said as he shuffled the papers, "that Brad knew Susie back in high school."

The air left Jamie's lungs. "Really?"

Nathan nodded. "They went to Cascia Hall together. Look." He dropped the papers and crossed the room, bending to one knee beside the chair. He slid one of the leather-bound volumes from the stack on the floor, opened it to the place a sticky note marked and handed it to Jamie.

It was a high-school yearbook. Among the rows of smiling black-and-white photos of seniors was a young cocky-looking Brad Alexander. And four rows below Brad, a young Susan Claremont.

"But you knew her back then, too, didn't you? So didn't you also know Brad?"

"Not until college. I'd see him at big parties, football games, stuff like that. I never realized he knew Susie."

"What makes you think they knew each other even if they went to the same high school?"

He stood and crossed back to the big desk. He switched on the green-hooded lamp. He picked up the papers again and returned to her with a small stack of bent and folded notes written on ruled notebook paper.

"These."

Jamie studied them. They were obviously child-ish crush notes—early high school maybe, judging by the content and the immature cant of the hand-writing—a roundish girlish hand, alternating with a tight spiked self-conscious masculine one. The notes were alternately signed S.C. and B.A. "Susie and Brad?"

He nodded. "Robert got bored a couple of days ago and asked permission to dig around in the boxes of family papers in the attic. There are tons. Mostly old tax records, oil royalty statements, newspaper clippings. He was hoping to find some of my mother's Hart stuff. He found these notes, instead. Well hidden."

"That's what you were doing the other night when I came by? Looking through these?"

He nodded with his eyes downcast.

"Nathan, I'm sorry you found these, but they were written by kids. They don't mean a thing."

"Except that she kept them."

"Maybe. Or maybe she just forgot she had them."

"And moved them here? After we were mar-ried?"

Nathan stood still for a moment before he added, "There are others. Why would she keep them all?"

Jamie couldn't answer that. "The real point is,

Brad—the man prosecuting you—knew her, and he hasn't been honest about that."

"Yes. If B.A., is in fact, Brad Alexander."

"And if Brad Alexander knew the victim in high school, wouldn't he be obligated to recuse himself?"

"Unless he had a reason, a motive, not to reveal their connection."

Jamie looked at the papers in her hand with dawning horror. Unless he was trying to frame Nathan. "What should we do now?"

Nathan looked at his watch. "Robert and I have to get back to Pawhuska and talk to the old guy before it gets too late. I know you have to go to work later, but in the meantime, could you do me a favor and see what you can find out about Brad's relationship with Susie?"

"You're not going to go to Van Horn with these?" She held up the notes.

He raised his eyebrows as if to say, *Get real.* "I'll need more than a few love notes with cryptic initials on them to link Brad with Susie. Without firm evidence, maybe even witnesses, Van Horn isn't going to pursue this. He'll ask Brad about it, and Brad will make some excuse about everybody in town knowing Susie Claremont or knowing of her. I think it'd be safer to wait and talk to Cynthia first thing Monday morning."

"Why wait till Monday?"

"She's already left town for the Thanksgiving weekend."

"Okay. I'll look into it." Jamie leafed through the notes quickly. "Do they mention any other kids in the notes? Anybody I might talk to?"

"No. But Susie knew Hunter and Andrea back in high school. Actually, she knew them…all her life." His voice caught.

"The Roths?" Jamie intentionally brought him back to the urgent problems of the present. "Your neighbors?"

Nathan nodded. "They knew Brad in high school, too."

The Roths. The lovely young couple with the slightly hostile attitude toward the media. Jamie wondered if they'd even deign to speak to her, but for Nathan's sake, she had to try.

CHAPTER THIRTEEN

JAMIE STEPPED UP onto the soaring Dallas-style front porch of the Roth home and rang the doorbell. It chimed in a series of tones that sounded exactly like Nathan's. Hunter answered in faded jeans, a threadbare University of Oklahoma sweatshirt and loafers without socks. "Ms. Evans," he said. "To what do I owe the pleasure?"

"Hello, Hunter. I was wondering if you and Andrea might have time to answer a few questions."

"Questions?"

"Off the record. I'm trying to help Nathan."

"Oh. We'll do anything we can to help Nathan."

He opened the door and let her enter.

"Why don't we sit in here?" He led her to the living room, where immaculate scrolled white woodwork, a soaring cathedral ceiling and lush pale carpeting sent the message *Formal! Don't dare relax.* The room featured banks of sunny windows similar to Nathan's. A Thanksgiving mantel arrangement twinkled with lights even at four o'clock in the afternoon. The air that moved serenely beneath a gigantic ceiling fan was perfumed with the best of holiday blends.

"Please sit down. Andrea's not here. Out with the kids somewhere. I was catching up on my office e-mail."

"Did I disturb your work?" Again Jamie wondered what his line of work was.

"No. It can wait. Now, what is this about?"

"A couple of things. How long have you and Andrea known Nathan and Susie?"

"We go way back. Since high school. Actually, we knew Susie in grade school. We all went to the same private school, Cascia Hall, but we didn't know Nathan until later, in college. He grew up out on that ranch, went to high school in Pawhuska."

"Tell me what Nathan was like back then." This question was more for her benefit than for Nathan's.

"In college? He was the all-American boy. Good-looking, popular, athletic, fun."

"And as a young man, was he ever violent, prone to losing his temper?"

"Nathan Hart Biddle?" Hunter drew the name out in disbelief. "There was never a more content easygoing guy. Honest, too. That's what's so disturbing about these murder charges. It simply could not be Nathan. The jury will see that. Cynthia's a fine lawyer. She'll get him off. You'll see.''

Jamie agreed, but she wondered if Hunter was trying to reassure her or himself. ''Would you say they had a good marriage?''

Hunter looked away for one split second before he insisted, ''The best.'' But facing Jamie's skeptical frown, he quickly vacillated. ''Okay, not the best, exactly. But it was as good as a marriage as could be with a woman like Susie.''

''A woman like Susie?''

''Susie could be a little, uh…difficult.''

''How so?''

''Ms. Evans—''

''Call me Jamie.''

''I don't see how personal information like this is going to help Nathan any. And besides, why don't you ask him if you want to know? I don't think it's my place to be speculating to the media about the Biddles' marriage. There's been quite enough of that already.''

''I have asked Nathan, and he's told me everything he knows, but I'm starting to form a different picture, a new theory, here. A theory that might save Nathan, but unfortunately it's one he might have difficulty proving…or even accepting.''

''What kind of theory?'' The sharp voice was Andrea's. She was standing behind them just inside a pair of French doors that opened into a long dining room. She held several department-store shopping bags in her arms, and behind her, a preteen boy and girl clutched more bags and stared.

"Sweetums!" Hunter jumped to his feet. "How'd the Christmas shopping go?"

"Fine." Andrea pivoted and thrust the bags into her son's arms. "You guys go upstairs and put this stuff away."

"Mom! Cut it out!" The son made a feint as if he might drop the bags. "Whaddaya mean, put it away? This stuff is for Christmas."

"I meant…put it on my bed. Then go into the upstairs den and watch TV until I call you for dinner."

They obeyed, albeit sulkily. Jamie heard the girl's awed voice drift down as they climbed the stairs: "Ted-dee, do you know who that is? Jamie Evans from Channel Six!"

"Big deal," her brother muttered.

Andrea sank into an armchair and assessed Jamie. "What's this theory of yours? And how will it help Nathan?"

"It could help establish motive, establish a suspect other than Nathan. In the majority of homicides, the victim knows the murderer. I want you to help me go back into Nathan and Susie's past. In particular, I want to know what you remember about Susie's relationship with a guy named Brad Alexander. He's the first assistant—"

"We know who he is," Hunter interjected.

Andrea pounced on her husband. "I knew this would happen."

Jamie felt prickles running up and down her spine.

"When we found out Brad was investigating Susie's murder, we thought it was strange. But he always was brilliant, the best. The very best and—"

"We figured it might even turn out to be a plus that he knew her. We figured it would make him doubly determined to solve the crime."

"I told you we should have come forward," Hunter muttered, and sank back onto the couch cushions.

"No!" Andrea stiffened, suddenly vehement.

"Come forward about what?"

The pair exchanged a look, then Andrea said, "All right. I'm sure it was nothing, but Brad and Susie did know each other. In fact, Brad had a crush on Susie."

"It was just a stupid high-school crush," Hunter added. "Practically every guy at Cascia Hall had a crush on Susie Claremont. She was gorgeous, you know. She, uh…developed early and all, had that, you know, certain ultrafeminine bearing. There was…just something about her."

"Hunter!"

He actually jumped. He'd seemed to have forgotten that his wife was in the room.

"For heaven's sake!" Andrea shot Jamie a nervous grin. "You sound like you had a crush on her yourself."

Jamie picked up the warning in the wife's tone.

Hunter swiveled his head toward his wife. His eyes widened. "Not I, sweetums. You know that. But old Brad certainly was crazy about her." Hunter shifted his body toward Jamie as if eliciting support. "Everybody knew that. That's why we figured if nobody else from our old crowd came forward, why in the world should we? The point is, if you're going to suspect Brad Alexander of…of something, then you'll have to cast suspicion on half the guys in the old school."

Andrea had continued to give her husband a warning glare while he spoke. Finally she turned her gaze to Jamie. "Whatever you do, you mustn't tell Nathan about this. It was all a long time ago, way before he met Susie, and Nathan has had enough heartache already. What good would it do for him to know that Brad, or any other guy for that matter, had a thing for Susie?"

"It might do him a lot of good!" Indignation shot through Jamie. How dare these people take it upon themselves to decide what information to keep from the officials! Especially when Nathan's life was at stake. "Alexander has no business working on this case. He could even be a suspect, can't you see that?''

At the word *suspect,* Hunter and Andrea leaned forward in one synchronized move. ''For heaven's sake, Ms. Evans,'' Andrea chastised. ''Don't let your reporter's imagination get carried away. Brad Alexander comes from a fine family, a genteel family. He's…he's very well educated and, well, he's no more a murderer than…than…''

''Than Nathan?'' Jamie could hardly control her frustration. ''You should have informed the police about this.''

''Have you ever considered the possibility that this information about Susie's background could actually weaken Nathan's case?'' Hunter argued. ''Make him look jealous and all?''

''I'll let Nathan be the judge of that.'' Jamie stood. ''I can find my way to the door.''

Andrea jumped up. ''I'll see you out. No trouble.''

When they got to the foyer, Andrea stepped out onto the front porch and pulled the door shut behind her. ''Ms. Evans.''

''Yes?''

''I want you to try to see something.''

''Okay.''

Andrea sighed and pulled her coat, which she hadn't bothered to remove, around her thin frame. ''Susie Biddle was a horrible, spoiled, manipulative—'' she shuddered ''—little bitch, and Nathan deserved better.''

Jamie let out a pent-up breath. Now at last maybe she was going to hear the truth. ''So there's more to the story of Brad and Susie?''

''Not really. He was simply another one of Susie's many flings, as far as I know.''

''Then what are you saying?''

''I'm saying, if you point the finger of suspicion at Brad Alexander, he's going to drag all the other guys into it.''

''All the other guys?''

''It was like a…a club. All the guys who'd been used and dumped by Susan Claremont and hated her for it.''

''I don't understand.''

''I'm trying to tell you what Susie was really like. She liked to keep all the boys—and I'm imagining later, all the men, too—on a string. Even after she'd dumped them. She was an incredible flirt. She wasn't happy unless she was breaking somebody's heart. She went after everybody's boyfriend,'' Andrea drew a huge resigned breath, ''including mine.''

''Hunter was involved with her?''

Andrea nodded. ''Yes. Now I hope you can see why this mustn't come out. What would that information do to Hunter and Nathan's friendship? And they *are* friends,'' she rushed on to elaborate, "good friends. Hunter thinks the world of Nathan. I do, too. For his sake, we tolerated Susie." She pressed two manicured fingers to her temple, composing herself. "And...and if the police knew Hunter had been involved with Susie in high school, they might even get the wrong idea about *him*. We have two children, Ms. Evans, and Hunter's juvenile fling with Susie was a long time ago."

"I'm sorry—"

"It doesn't matter." She waved off Jamie's pity. "Hunter is a grown-up now...sort of."

"That's not what I meant," Jamie said quickly. She paused for a moment, then continued, "Look, I can understand that you don't want your husband dragged into this, but—"

"No! You don't understand!" Andrea cried.

"*What* don't I understand?" Jamie sensed the woman's panic.

"Hunter can't...he can't be dragged into this. His work is too..."

"What does he do?"

"Politics." Andrea raised her chin. "He's a consultant. A very skilled consultant. He's just beginning to make his mark." Andrea bit her lip. "And this stupid thing with Susie—"

"But you just said his involvement with Susie was a juvenile fling that happened a long time ago," Jamie argued. "Why would it hurt his career now?"

"He wrote notes to her. Silly, obsessive love letters. We don't even know where they are."

Jamie sucked in a breath. *She* knew.

Andrea closed her eyes and sighed dramatically. "In the political world, perception is everything. Just being questioned by the police might ruin Hunter's career. I'm sure Brad has the same fear." Andrea clutched Jamie's arm with her thin fingers.

"Please," she pleaded. "Before you go off on some hysterical tangent about all these meaningless high-school crushes... Why, I doubt Susie and Brad ever even saw each other again after high school."

But Jamie suspected they *had* seen each other, because a disturbing memory was already eating at her mind. "Excuse me." She removed Andrea's hand. "I've got to go now." She turned and hurried to her car. She had to get back to the station and pull up the exact piece of tape that was worrying her.

CHAPTER FOURTEEN

WHY HADN'T SHE seen it before? Jamie used the AVID software to enhance her subject, a lanky blond man far back in the crowd, standing with his foot braced against the rear bumper of a red Jeep. She locked on and brought Brad Alexander's features into sharper focus. She reached for the phone, dialed Nathan's number while she studied the emotions on that magnified face. Jealousy. And naked painful longing. She got no answer at the ranch house and remembered that Nathan and Robert had gone back into Pawhuska to talk to that old Osage one more time. She tried Nathan's cell phone, but only got his voice mail. Maybe he was out of range.

Frustrated at having to leave such a sensitive message on a cell phone, she chose her words carefully, "Nathan, it's Jamie. I'm looking at a piece of tape from four years ago—that celebrity golf tournament where you rode the horse. You've got to see this. There's a face in the crowd... Call me as soon as you get this message. Something about this whole setup gives me the heebie-jeebies."

Next she tried calling Cynthia. Gone for the Thanksgiving weekend, she remembered. But just to be sure, she left an answering machine message at her office, too. Maybe Cynthia could demand that Van Horn take Brad off this case.

The longer she looked at the tormented face on the screen, the more frightened she became. Maybe she shouldn't wait. She checked her watch. Four fifty-five already, but if she was lucky, she could still catch Van Horn. She punched in the number.

"Trent. Jamie Evans." The stunned silence on the other end of the phone told Jamie that Van Horn sensed something was up.

"Yes?"

"Are you alone?" That question would really spook him, but he sounded as if he was on a speakerphone.

"What is this about, Ms. Evans?" There was irritation in his voice.

"I have some new information in the Biddle case. Very important information, I think."

"Which is?"

"Not on the phone."

"Ms. Evans, if you have some new evidence, we may need to take your statement. And that requires skilled personnel. Can't this wait until Monday? It's already—" she imagined him checking his Rolex watch "—four fifty-five and I—"

"No. It can't wait. I think you need to hear about this right now."

"Then get over here. Quickly please. I was on my way to a function."

AS SOON AS Trent hit the disconnect button, Brad spoke. "That woman—" he pointed at the speakerphone "—is heavily involved with the accused."

"So you told me."

"Whatever she has to say is suspect."

"True." Trent paced to the window and fidgeted with his Rolex.

"Boss, listen, you're already running late. It's not going to do us any good to get this conviction if you don't keep your mind on getting elected next spring. You go on. I'll see what Ms. Evans has to say."

"I appreciate that, Brad. I don't know what I'd have done without you these last few weeks. This Biddle case has been driving me nuts."

"Don't mention it. I'll concentrate on getting this conviction. You concentrate on getting yourself reelected. Your job security is my job security, too, after all."

IN THE TANGLE of rush-hour traffic, Jamie gripped the steering wheel as if squeezing it harder would make her arrive at the DA's office faster. Her own stupidity—her blindness—made her want to strangle something, and she repeatedly twisted her fingers around the wheel in frustration. She only hoped Van Horn would wait for her, but her hopes dimmed when she turned the Channel Six news wagon into an empty parking garage. Even the security guard in the little ticket booth had left. But of course, it was the Wednesday before the Thanksgiving holiday, and no self-respecting bureaucrat would stay one millisecond after five o'clock. She parked near the elevators, anyway, and rode up, hoping that maybe Trent was doing his job for once and dogging this case.

She whipped her cell phone out of her shoulder bag as the elevator doors opened—and then her heart plummeted.

Brad Alexander, looking cool and composed in a fashionable chestnut suit, cream shirt and matching tie stood silhouetted in the darkened reception area.

"Ms. Evans." He approached her calmly.

"Hi, Brad." She stepped forward, grateful that her experience in front of the camera had trained her to act confident even when her knees were threatening to buckle.

"What can I do for you?"

"Is Trent still around?"

"No. He asked me to help you. Why don't you step into my office?" He extended a hand in that direction.

Jamie didn't want to arouse his suspicions, so she didn't hesitate, walking a few steps ahead of him, while her mind scrambled for an exit plan. Too late, she realized she should have arranged to meet Van Horn in a neutral place, away from these offices.

As soon as she entered his office, Brad closed the door and Jamie thought she saw him flip a button on the knob. The wide wooden blinds over the picture window were open, but no lamps were lit, so that the room glowed dimly with the waning evening light. ''Trent told me that you think you have some kind of new evidence in the Biddle case.'' Brad spoke smoothly as he rounded his massive desk and seated himself.

Jamie surveyed her surroundings while her reporter's mind recorded unsettling details: the pretentious rich décor; a wall of diplomas, awards and certificates in identical guilt frames; a sterile desktop with—her heart did a tumble—a mug shot of Nathan Biddle squared precisely on top of a stack of files.

Unfortunately her reporter's mind refused to come up with a quick way out of this situation without arousing Brad's suspicions. Brad indicated a chair for her. She ignored the gesture and stayed close to the door.

''I don't want to take up your time, Brad. I really came to talk to Trent. In fact, the whole thing can wait until after Thanksgiving. Just tell him I came by." She put her hand on the knob.

"He authorized me to handle this. Now, what is this new evidence?" He pulled a ballpoint pen and a legal pad from a drawer.

Jamie found the door locked and her heart drummed a warning.

Without looking up, Brad said, "It's automatic. For security. Now, the evidence?"

Jamie eyed him. His jaw flexed as he clicked the ballpoint up and down repeatedly while arranging the tablet precisely in the center of the desk blotter, waiting for her answer. She could feel the tension and temper that frequently swirled around Brad Alexander.

"The evidence?" He poised the pen. "It is, I assume, not the kind of evidence that will help us get a conviction."

Jamie licked her lips and her throat went dry. "Ah...well, I don't know. It's actually kind of insignificant." Her mind did a quick scan, looking for some plausible irrelevancy to feed him.

"Come on, Ms. Evans. Why would you bring us something that would incriminate him? I am an investigator, remember? It's common knowledge that you have allowed yourself to become... involved with Mr. Biddle."

Jamie felt a second of shock, realizing Brad knew about her and Nathan. She shook it off and concentrated on Brad's every move, his every inflection. She thought it strange that he would call Nathan Mr. Biddle when he had apparently known the Biddles socially. Maybe she was putting too much emphasis on that, which was what Andrea Roth had claimed.

"You know them? The Biddles, I mean?" It was a test.

Brad stopped clicking the pen and suspended it over the legal pad for a long moment before he started making random marks on the paper. "The clever little investigative reporter. And what if I did know them? The bastard is still guilty."

The bastard? Brad's hostility, it seemed, had suddenly flared and focused on a target. Why hadn't she seen this before? She ground her teeth, angry for allowing herself to be used to settle some kind of ancient grudge that Brad Alexander held against Nathan Biddle. It probably went back to the days when Brad had lost to Nathan Biddle in the contest for Susie Claremont's affections. "I don't think he's guilty, Brad."

"Oh, really?" The random marks became longer slashes. *Jzzit. Jzzit. Jzzit.* The pen was actually shredding the paper. "Your opinion doesn't count for much. Like I said, anyone can see that you're infatuated with Biddle, but even so, I'm curious. How the hell can you defend a man who would kill his pregnant wife?"

Jamie's heart did a sickening somersault. Nathan should have been the only one who knew Susie was pregnant. She recalled the argument she had with Nathan over his stubborn decision to keep that information secret, even from his attorney. He said he'd never told anyone, not even Robert. And she knew *she* hadn't let it slip to anyone. The pen continued to make rapid slashing sounds in the silence. With his back to the windows, Jamie couldn't read Brad's face in the fading evening light, but she didn't need to. Each stroke of the pen grew more violent, telling her how agitated he was becoming.

"She was pregnant?"

The pen stilled. And even in the darkness, Brad's face appeared to pale. His eyes shifted up, then away. When he stood abruptly, Jamie braced her back against the door, but Brad spun away from her, toward the windows. He crossed his arms over his chest and stuck his hands under his armpits, his shoulders bunching with tension inside the tailored suit. Through the slats of the blinds, the dying sun made grotesque stripes across one side of his tortured face.

"She was," Brad finally said, "but I'm the only one who knew it—besides, of course, her sorry husband." Then he added, very softly, "And, of course, now *you* know."

Fear coiled in Jamie's gut, but she fought to stay calm. How on earth did this damn door unlock?

Now that he'd made this tactical error, there was no telling what Brad might do. Part of her still wanted to believe she was trapped in this room with a vengeful but righteous assistant DA, not a murderer. Maybe there was a logical explanation for how he'd gotten that information. Maybe it somehow came out in his investigation. "I don't understand. How did you know she was pregnant?"

"Because—" he turned and she could see a fine sheen of sweat forming on his face "—I was the father."

Jamie sucked in a breath and could only shake her head in horrified disbelief. In the gloomy light she saw Brad's face transform. His expression took on a weird quality. He looked triumphant, proud...and suddenly quite insane.

"That's how I know he did it, Ms. Evans. I know his motives better than anyone."

"I don't understand," she said, stalling while behind her back, her hands fumbled. The knob wasn't a simple turn-and-push lock, and her fingers groped for the elusive release button.

"Don't you get it?" Brad's crazy eyes glowed in the slanted sunlight. "Susie Biddle and I were having an affair. We were very much in love. She was trying to figure out a way to tell Biddle about us when she...when she became pregnant. Something her own husband couldn't do for her, I'm afraid. Susie knew the pregnancy would throw Biddle into a rage. I realize he's got you fooled, Ms. Evans, but Nathan Biddle is a very dangerous man. Anyway, Susie decided it would be best if Biddle believed the child was his—the Biddle fortune and the Hart family's oil head rights were at stake, after all, and Susie was used to fine things. But more than anything she was just plain afraid of him. She convinced me that we could be comfortably wealthy and still have our child. I, of course—'' his voice rose ''—never approved of that idea.''

Jamie had been a reporter long enough to sense the twists and turns of an on-the-spot lie. The scary part was, Brad seemed to be warming to his own delusional story, becoming more convinced as he made it up.

''Oh, no. *I* wanted her to…I urged her, begged her, to break it off with him immediately.'' Brad's jaw clenched and when he looked over his shoulder at her, Jamie noticed a vein down the center of his forehead bulging with tension. ''But Susie convinced me that it would be safer if Biddle never knew about me, and…and then she…she promised that as soon as the child was born, she would divorce Biddle.''

Jamie wondered how she was ever going escape from this madman.

''But Biddle must have discovered the truth that

night. Or maybe Susie simply decided to tell him the truth. I doubt that, though. She would have told me. We were so close, you know. Maybe they argued and he simply killed her in a blind rage. Maybe he came back from Bartlesville and killed her in cold blood. I don't know. All I know for sure is that the bastard disposed of the woman I loved and then faked her disappearance.''

Jamie had to think of a way to keep him talking. As long as he was ranting like this, she might have a chance to escape. ''Why haven't you come forward with this story?'' she asked.

''Who would have believed me? And what good would it do to destroy Susie's reputation and throw her grieving family into a turmoil of scandal? At first I even wondered if she had disappeared in order to get away from her violent husband. I hoped so.'' Brad's speech was more rapid, more pressured now, and spittle leaked from the corner of his mouth. ''Can you imagine how I felt? Watching that creep mourn his missing wife on TV every night when I was the one who had lost the woman I love.'' Tears of self-pity actually glimmered in Brad's eyes as he fell silent.

Shocked and sickened by this display, Jamie stood with her hand clutching the still-locked doorknob, thinking, *If Susie Biddle was really your lover and she had gone into hiding, she would have*

*contacted you, and in a second you're going to
figure out your own screwup.*

She started to shake, wondering how the murder
had actually happened, how Brad had killed Susie.
Choking back a squeak of terror, she turned and
finally found the button to release the lock.

But before she could yank the door open, Brad
leaped across the room and grabbed her by the
shoulders, spinning her around, pinning her against
the wall. "You don't believe me, do you?" he
shouted. "You're just like Susie! Blinded by his
good looks!"

Jamie's insides turned to ice while Alexander
kept shaking her, repeating, "You're...exactly...
like...*her!*"

She gained enough wits to scream, "Stop it!"

He froze, his face contorted. It was as if he'd
snapped back to reality, back from the fantasy he'd
created. "I didn't mean to hurt her," he pleaded,
"don't you see?" His fingers dug more deeply into
Jamie's shoulders. "I took her out to the cabin to
help her, console her."

"The cabin?" Jamie whispered in growing disbelief. "The old cabin on Hart Ranch?"

"It wasn't my idea. That's where she wanted to
go. She called me. Crying. Biddle had hurt her
again. She actually begged him to stay in town that
night. But Biddle had a big business meeting in
Kansas City. He was always breaking her heart like

that. And then she'd turn to me. And I was always there for her. Just like that night.''

Jamie wondered what part of this version was a lie, too, but Brad's new story matched Nathan's—except that Nathan had never mentioned Brad Alexander. Because Nathan had never even been aware that this pathetic man had been a part of his late wife's life. ''Brad...'' Jamie tried to twist his hands from her shoulders, but he only tightened his grip.

Face-to-face, the coldness and irrationality in Brad's eyes paralyzed her. ''I was in love with her a long time before that bastard even knew her,'' he stated, ''and I would never have done anything to hurt her. We just had too much wine, that's all. She was so despondent and desperate when I got to the mansion I thought for sure she'd leave him this time. But then she told me she was pregnant.'' He choked on his dry sobs. ''And how her own husband didn't care enough to stay in town and take care of her.''

Staring into Brad's contorted face, she saw again the frozen video frame of him at the golf tournament. And suddenly, as plain as if she were looking right at the monitor, she saw something she had missed before. The license plate on that Jeep he was leaning against was a vanity plate that read 1-ASST—for First Assistant, she supposed. The old man at the nursing home had been rambling about a "one ass" when his granddaughter had interfered. They never got the full story from the old man, but Jamie knew she had it now.

The old man had seen Brad's vanity plates when he rented the boat to take Susie Biddle's body out to an island in the Arkansas River. An image of Nathan's leather jacket crossed Jamie's mind. How had Brad gotten that jacket? What had happened that night?

"She ran from me in the dark...." Brad's voice trailed off in sorrow. When his grip relaxed, Jamie's hand crept back to the knob. But Brad's grief wasn't so great that he didn't notice. He stopped her with one swift smack.

Her hand flew to her stinging jaw.

"Don't try that again," he warned her calmly, any sign of sadness suddenly gone. He jerked her away from the door and dragged her by the wrist to his desk, where he yanked open a drawer, producing a gun.

"Come on." He waved the weapon, pointing the barrel at her, then at the door. "Let's go."

"Where are we going?"

"Your car."

"Where are you taking me?"

His smile was smooth, malicious. "Hart Ranch, of course. I'm afraid your boyfriend is going to strike again."

The interior of the service elevator was lit by

only one weak bulb, and by the time doors opened in the parking garage, Jamie had managed to slide her keys and clicker from the side pocket of her shoulder bag into her hand.

As soon as her car was within range, she hit the panic button. In that first second of alarm when the bleating horn created a din in the cavernous concrete garage, Jamie tore loose and dashed to the stairwell. But Brad's legs were too long, too fast. He caught her on the second stair. Before he could wrest the keys from her hand and silence the car alarm, Jamie flung them down a nearby drainage grate.

Brad stopped struggling and stared at the bars of the grate, narrowly spaced and set in solid concrete. He shook her violently, shouting, "Where's your spare set?" above the jarring repetitions of the alarm.

"Don't have one." Jamie gave him a cold stare and tried to twist free.

"Fine. Then you've just complicated things nicely." He maintained his grip and poked the gun into her side as he dragged her forward. "I was going to let you die an accidental death in your own car, but now—"

"Let me go, Brad."

"Sorry. Can't. We'll figure out how he abducted you and got you to the ranch later."

"Why the ranch?"

"Why not?" He was shouting over the sound of the car alarm as he pushed her along toward a sedan parked in a dark corner. "The place is isolated. It's his territory. He's a madman. Don't forget, Trent thinks you've just given me some new evidence. When I relay that evidence—and I'll make sure it's enough to seal Biddle's fate—to the police, it's only a matter of time before we find your body wherever Biddle has hidden it. You see how it all fits, don't you? Then, we find your car in the parking garage with the battery dead from the alarm going off for hours—"

"What if the cops show up and check out that alarm right now?"

"Not likely. Thanksgiving break. Downtown is already dead. But even if they do, you're gone. Biddle has intercepted you. I'm going to say I tried to get you to wait for a security escort to the garage, but you left my office in a big hurry to get back to the station and get this new development ready to go on the ten-o'clock news. Unfortunately that's all I'm going to know."

"What if Nathan has an alibi?"

"His cousin Robert? That's who he's with right now, you know. I've kept close track. Easy enough. He's the accused."

"But then the people tailing him would know—"

"Thanks for the reminder." He brought her up

short and flipped a cell phone out of his pocket. He punched in a number as he poked the gun in her side, forcing her to keep moving. As they hurried along in the dark garage, she heard him give instructions to someone to stop tailing Biddle and return to Tulsa for the night. He said he had new evidence he needed him to look into. She heard the phone beep off.

"The DA's district investigator," Brad explained calmly. "My timing will have to be impeccable, but then, it always is. In the meantime here we are." They had reached Brad's shiny red BMW. No vanity plates on his new car, Jamie noted. She looked around for a place to run, to hide. But the garage was barren, open.

She hoped the curb was stenciled with a job title, like the ones around it, hoped it had FIRST ASSISTANT DA on it. While he dug out his keys and opened the car, she reached back and unclipped her pager from her belt. "And now, of course," Brad said, "I am about to leave the building—alone." As he pushed her to the seat, bending her head forward, Jamie dropped her arm and slid the pager onto the concrete under the car.

"Stay down and don't pull anything cute," Alexander warned. "I'd hate to have to shoot you in my new car. Messy."

Jamie felt the twisting and turning of the car through downtown Tulsa, then the incline and acceleration as they climbed an entrance ramp onto the interstate. She fought down her panic, trying to think how she might save herself. If someone found her pager…but then what? Maybe they'd put out an APB on Alexander's car. Her cell phone made a resonant tone when she turned it on, so even if she could get her hand in her bag and punch out a number, he'd snatch it away before she could reach anyone. But there was always Dave. When he came in to transfer footage for the ten-o'clock news, he'd see the monitor in the editing bay, right on the frame where she left it—on Brad's disturbed face. But would Dave figure out what that meant? And even if the police figured out she was with Alexander, how would they know where he'd taken her? Maybe later she could page herself and punch in the ranch number on her digital pager. *Please, God, let someone find it.*

For now, all she could do was wait…and pray.

CHAPTER FIFTEEN

"MR. PRETTYWATER," Robert said gently, "why did you and your friend call the rude young man who knocked over your domino game 'one ass'?"

Nathan would give Robert one thing, he had the patience of Job. This was his third trip, Nathan's second, to the Pawhuska Nursing Home, and every time they'd plowed the same old ground. But today they were finally getting somewhere. Mr. Prettywater seemed more alert and talkative than usual. And there was no protective granddaughter in sight.

"Because it was right there on the guy's license plate."

Nathan and Robert glanced at each other and leaned forward, all ears.

The old man grew more animated. "Wc watched him out the front window of the store. He drove off with that canoe all cattywhompus, lashed to the top of that fancy Jeep. And he had that license plate that said 'one'—" the old man made a mark in the air with his arthritic finger, like the numeral one "—and 'A-S-S.'" He enunciated each letter.

"A-S-S?" Nathan questioned.

"I know. Sounds crazy, but if Charlie was alive he'd tell you. That's exactly what it said. And Charlie, he was such a cutup, he said, 'That fella's a number-one ass if I ever saw one.'" The old fellow chuckled and gave his leg a feeble slap. "We made a running joke out of it after that, you know? Every time I'd be winning at Moon, Charlie'd say, 'Where's old one ass when I need him?'" The old man gave another wheezing guffaw, while Robert and Nathan exchanged puzzled looks over his head.

"You're sure that's what the license said, Mr. Prettywater?"

"'Course I'm sure. I'm old, but I ain't addled."

Driving back to Tulsa, Nathan and Robert tried to make sense of it.

"That's a weird thing to put on your license plate, one ass."

"But that should make it easier to track down with the Department of Motor Vehicles." Nathan pulled out his cell phone and placed a call to Frank. "He'll run the check for anything along those lines now," he said when he was finished talking. "The sooner we find that Jeep, the sooner we find the owner." He punched another number into the phone. "I'm gonna call Jamie and tell her. She might know something after talking to Hunter and Andrea.''

Robert grinned. "You just like to talk to that woman every thirty minutes.''

THE RANCH WAS deserted, as Jamie had feared it would be.

The BMW skidded as it cut fresh tracks in the snow, climbing the road that rose toward the ruins of Grandfather's cabin.

"Tell me again what happened," she said, hoping that getting Brad to talk about it would make him emotional again and maybe careless enough to allow her to escape. "After the two of you got to the cabin?''

"Like I told you—'' Brad concentrated on his driving as he talked "—we had too much to drink. Susie loved me—she was just confused. When I tried to kiss her, she pushed me away. I knew she really wanted me, but when I tried to give her what she wanted, she acted like I was trying to rape her or something. I could not believe it when she grabbed that old knife—''

"The one the police found?''

"Wasn't that extremely lucky?'' Brad smiled, but then his face hardened into a diabolical mask. "That old Indian's knife. She grabbed it off the mantel. I tried to get it away from her without hurting her—self-defense, don't you see?—and she cut me. Bad. Across my arm. My blood dripped everywhere. I had to use my tie to bind it. That's why—'' he cast her a sly look ''—the jacket.''

''The jacket?''

''I had to have the leather jacket to cover my arm. It was amazing how it fell right into my plan later. I wasn't even aware of the logo that night. The coat was merely a convenience at the time.''

Jamie looked at his profile in horror. ''And that's why you set the fire that burned the cabin.''

''You *are* clever, Ms. Evans.'' He glanced at her. Jamie had never seen such cold blue eyes. ''I couldn't have the cops getting wise and spraying Luminol all over the place, finding DNA that wasn't Nathan Biddle's—*my* DNA, in fact—way out here. They didn't spray the cabin when she disappeared. It was so isolated and there were no tire tracks. I took care of that. Even so—'' Brad seemed proud of this part ''—it took some pretty fancy footwork to keep them away. I doubt I could have done it this time.''

''You must have had a busy night.''

''Exhausting.'' He didn't seem to grasp the horror of what he had done or was about to do. Jamie had a sense of the surreal as, instead of going up to the cabin ruins, they turned off onto the narrow icy gravel road that led to the base of the cliff.

''This is where she fell,'' Brad said when he stopped the car.

Jamie stared through the windshield. Fresh snow had started to come down, and as it stuck to the wall of the cliff, it made the rocks look like…a grouping of long faces. "I don't understand."

"After I cut her in the struggle, trying to get the knife away from her, she ran out into the dark. She fell off this cliff, broke her neck."

Through her revulsion, Jamie thought she heard tears in his voice. Maybe she could take advantage of his emotional state.

"Then…you didn't kill her," she said quietly. "It was an accident, Brad."

"That's what I've been telling you!" he shrieked.

"All we have to do is go back to Tulsa. Let me call someone. Let me get you some help. You need help, Brad. You didn't kill her. It was an accident. You loved her. You shouldn't have to suffer like this. We can get you help."

"And what about him? He just gets off scot-free? He *caused* her death! Don't you see that? I had no choice but to frame him once her body had been found."

"I can see that you were desperate, Brad. You weren't yourself. No one is going to blame you for an accident."

But Brad didn't seem to hear. He got out and stumbled past the headlights and jerked her from the passenger door onto the packed snow. He pushed her to her knees and pressed the barrel of the gun to her temple. "Sorry, Ms. Evans," he hissed, "but you should have minded your own business, instead of mucking around for the sake of that bastard."

Jamie heart rioted and she squeezed her eyes shut. Tears burned as she thought of her sweet parents, who had wanted her to be a schoolteacher, not a television reporter out confronting the ugly world. Had wanted her to marry nice safe Donald. Automatically her lips began silently saying the Hail Mary, exactly as she had always been taught.

Brrring! It was her cell phone, still in her tote on the floor of the car.

"Leave it!" Brad hissed.

Brrring! "Voice mail will get it on the fourth ring. I know. I've called you enough times."

Brrring!

After it rang a fourth time, Brad shoved Jamie forward, and she caught herself on her palms in the snow, too weak with fear to get up or even move.

Brad dug around in her tote for the phone. "Here." He thrust it under her face. "Check your messages. Give it to me after you enter your pass code."

Jamie did so with shaky fingers.

Brad ripped the phone from her hand and listened. Jamie could overhear Nathan's deep voice, but it was so mechanically distant on the phone that she couldn't make out the words. After listening for a minute a look of cunning hatred crossed Brad's face.

He gave her a nasty squint and punched off. ''Your boyfriend got your earlier message,'' he said mildly. ''He seemed pretty upset about my relationship with Susie. Well, I can put him out of his misery.'' Brad sighed and his voice dripped with phony regret. ''And now it looks like I'm gonna have to make a stop in Pawhuska after I'm finished with you both. Can't have that old fella testifying.''

Jamie's heart froze. Mr. Prettywater. Nathan's message must has mentioned whatever the sweet old gent had told him and Robert.

Brad emitted a short eerie high-strung laugh. ''What am I doing?'' his voice cracked with emotion. ''Biddle wouldn't kill you *here*. And certainly not with my gun! I must really be losing it. We can do better than this.''

He prodded Jamie to get her up and back into the car, then he drove down the gravel road toward the barn.

The blazing outdoor lights in the barnyard did nothing to reassure Jamie. Her eyes blurred as she tried to orient herself, to think, to hold on to hope. She knew that Nathan's hired hand, Charlie, drove over from his own place five miles away at dawn every day. But by now he'd been gone for several hours.

Brad dragged her from the car again and kept the gun pointed at her while he slid the massive barn door open a couple of feet. He poked her with the barrel, forcing her into the dark interior. The smell of hay, horseflesh and Brad's sweaty desperation filled her nostrils. The horses started whinnying and moving about in their stalls at the creepy intrusion.

She tried to pull away, but Brad grabbed her. He pressed an arm around her middle and dragged her backward. While she listened to the door inching closed behind her, she wondered if she should attempt to talk him down. She felt his frantic movements against her back, and from somewhere on his person, he produced a high-intensity penlight and switched it on.

Next he dug Jamie's cell phone from his jacket. "Call your boyfriend." He shoved her away, held the phone out and aimed the gun squarely into her face with the other hand.

Jamie looked at the gun, then into Brad's cold blue eyes. In the weird underlighting he looked totally crazed. "And say what?"

"The truth, my dear. Go ahead and tell him I've got you at the barn. Tell him to rush to the ranch to save you. According to his message, he's not far away."

"Why? So you can kill him, too?"

"Regrettable."

"And what about Robert? His cousin never leaves his side these days."

"Then I suppose Robert gets a bullet, too. I've got plenty."

Jamie looked at the cell phone. In the narrow shaft of the little penlight, Brad probably wouldn't be able to tell what number she was dialing. She could call Nathan and summon him the way Brad wanted her to, but that would put him and Robert in jeopardy. She could dial her pager, maybe have enough time before Brad caught on to punch in the ranch number as a signal to the police—*if* they'd found the pager by now. Jamie made her decision and took the phone.

She punched Nathan's number, at worst, she'd get his voice mail and at least create some kind of record, but Nathan's live voice answered. "Nathan! Listen!" she spoke rapidly. "Go back and guard Mr. Prettywater! Brad knows about him and he's going to ki—"

Since she had never even come close to passing out in her life, Jamie didn't recognize the signs. She'd always thought it was a sudden thing. But as soon as she felt the blow, time shifted into a sickening slow motion. Brad's enraged cursing distorted into a distant echo, and her vision telescoped to utter darkness as the rough barn floorboards zoomed toward her face.

WHILE HE FRANTICALLY punched in Jamie's cellphone number, Nathan shouted at Robert, "Turn around. That was Jamie and I think Alexander's got her."

"Turn around? Here?" The highway was narrow, dark and the snow on the shoulders stood two feet high.

"*Now,* dammit!"

Robert wheeled Nathan's Durango off onto the snowy shoulder. The tires gripped beautifully, he cut a hard turnabout, and they were back on the pavement in seconds.

Nathan gave up on getting Jamie to answer. He dialed 911, was patched through by the dispatcher to Jack Bates himself and quickly told the sheriff the whole story.

"Don't worry," Jack reassured him. "Be looking for our lights. We'll probably pass you on the way to the ranch."

"I doubt that. Robert's driving."

"And where am I going?" Robert said as he gained speed.

"Back to the ranch."

"Why there?"

"In the background, before Jamie got cut off, I

heard horses whinnying. I'd know Sweetie Pie anywhere, even over a cell phone."

Robert pushed the pedal to the floor.

Nathan punched in another number. "Dave? You seen Jamie around?"

Dave righted his chair from two legs to four, suddenly alert. It was a good thing he automatically answered this phone in the editing bay, instead of ignoring it like some of the photographers did. Nathan sounded really worried. "Jamie? No. We've been trying to page her, but she doesn't answer. We can't figure this out."

He listened to Nathan's next question while he fiddled with the AVID controls. He brought the tape back to where Jamie had left it. "Nope. She didn't say. But she left an enhanced segment up. She pulled it off a piece of tape I shot a few years ago. She looks at that tape a lot, and when I first walked in here, I thought, not again, but this time it looks like she zeroed in on something new. It's usually your pretty face, my man... Okay. But you're not gonna like this... Hey! How'd you know? And he looks really weird, man. Kinda psycho, if you ask me... Whaddaya mean, where was this taken? I guess he's at that golf tournament where you rode a horse all over the place. He's just standing there with his foot propped on the bumper of a Jeep... Hey, no problem. I can enhance almost any detail now. Hold on... Got it. It says, one—that's a numeral—then A-S-S-T. Oh, I get it. First Assistant. What a freaking egomaniac.''

Dave tapped the pencil while Nathan explained what the old Osage in Pawhuska had told them. Halfway through the story Dave's pencil froze. "Shit!" he interrupted. "I just remembered something! That day when they issued the search warrant at your Tulsa place? Brad came out and shook my hand and his was like, all gritty. I bet I've got a close-up of his hands on film, because he waved them right at the camera, and I bet those puppies are dirty. Oh man! I'm so stupid! The painter! The guy said something about a skinny blond dude— and I knew that had to be Alexander at the time— the painter said he'd been there early, prowling around the grounds. What the hell could he have been doing? Of course!" Dave snapped the pencil in two. "The bastard was out there planting that knife.''

"DAVE'S GONNA CALL the cops," Nathan said. "He and Jamie know the detective who worked Susie's murder." As soon as he'd punched off, he'd started dialing again. Jamie's cell phone, Robert assumed. And again, he apparently got no answer.

"Damn!" Nathan tossed the phone onto the dash, closed his eyes, and pinched the bridge of his nose. "I can't lose her, Robert.''

Robert accelerated even more. They were flying down an icy, twisting county road just north of Pawhuska at an unthinkable speed, but it was far more frightening to imagine Jamie in Brad Alexander's hands, or what would become of Nathan if anything happened to Jamie Evans.

Nathan opened his eyes and stared at the slushy blacktop whizzing away beneath their tires. His expression, at first desperate, became spellbound. He stared as if in a trance, and the way he looked gave Robert a funny feeling.

Robert couldn't decide what to do. He didn't want to let Nathan go off some deep end, but if he was having a vision, Robert didn't want to jar him out of it. After all, it could be something that might save Jamie's life. He wished he had the old shaman right here inside the Durango, riding with them. He looked out over the endless snow-covered brush at the roadside, revealed in the headlights and gone, revealed and gone. Snow. The snow had come, yet Nathan was not free like the eagle as the shaman had predicted. Every time he dared to take his eyes off the road and glanced over at Nathan, his cousin's eyes seemed wider, stranger, more fixed. No, Nathan was not free. In fact, he was trapped in a worse hell, now that he'd let himself fall in love again. Nathan's eyes, distant and fierce, filled Robert with fear.

Robert's heart started to beat like a drum with that fear, but he made himself wait. He drove and waited and asked the Great Spirit to help Nathan. He asked, also, for protection for Jamie Evans.

JAMIE CAME TO when the penlight blazed across her eyelids. When she opened her eyes, Brad aimed the light away and panned the tall rafters, the floor, the stalls. Then the beam froze on a familiar object that sent a chill up Jamie's spine. She sat up and the back of her head felt like a vise had gripped it.

"Perfect," Brad muttered under his breath. He yanked her to her feet and shoved her forward.

"What are you going to do? Strangle me?" Jamie asked as they moved closer to the coil of rope hanging beside the loft ladder.

"No, sweetheart. Don't be ridiculous. Your insane boyfriend is going to push you over the edge of that loft up there. And then when I get him up there and shoot him, he'll spin over the edge, too. I'll make sure he goes over. I can claim that it all happened any way I want. Come on. We don't have much time." He raised the light of the beam to the hayloft thirty feet in the air.

"COUSIN!" ROBERT CALLED out. He was down on one knee with a flashlight, examining tire tracks they'd spotted in the snow on the cabin road. They had come to the fork in that road—one direction led up to the plateau, the other down to the barn.

As he stood at the base of the cliff, Nathan fought the chilling nausea that lingered from the vision. The reappearance of the faces again had shaken his confidence. Should he and Robert drive up there to the top of that cliff? He could see the snow-covered rock formations that looked like faces. Was Jamie up there? Is that what the vision meant? But it would take time to drive up the narrow gravel road and back down again, and he'd clearly heard the horses when Jamie had called. He made up his mind and trotted over to Robert.

"Our tracks." Robert pointed. "And these are his. A double set, one going up and one heading back down toward the barns."

Nathan said, "Let's go to the barn." They ran to the Durango and followed the slushy trail down. Snow drifted into the open truck window with the wind, and then Nathan heard the sound he'd been listening for: horses whinnying.

"Kill the engine!"

Robert doused the headlights and threw the Durango into neutral. Now the only sound was of the big tires crunching snow as they rolled down the narrow road. The faint whinny of horses came drifting up again.

"Look!" Robert said.

There in the yardlights, standing out against the snow like a dark bloodstain, they spotted Brad's red BMW.

"Stop here in the trees," Nathan said.

"Right."

Robert braked the truck, grabbed the cell phone off the dash and punched 911, while Nathan jumped out and crossed the snowy barnyard on the shadowed side, as quiet as a panther stalking a kill.

As BRAD SHOVED Jamie toward the loft ladder on the opposite side of the barn, Jamie wondered if she could somehow elude him in the dark, release the horses or something. Create confusion. Anything.

But when she tried to break free, Brad wrenched her backward by her blouse, tearing off buttons and nearly choking her. "If you fight me," he breathed in her ear, "if it looks like there was a struggle, that will only make the whole thing all the more convincing."

Jamie coughed and gulped for breath. "Please," she gasped. "Don't do this."

"You've given me no choice." He forced her onto the first step of the ladder. "You should never have started digging around in something that was none of your business."

"Brad, I told you. I see now that Susie's death was a horrib—" she coughed again "—a horrible accident. Involuntary manslaughter. The police will see that, too.''

"Don't be ridiculous. No one will believe Susie took a knife to me just because I tried to kiss her. Now move.''

But Jamie stayed where she was. "I believe you! You're the respected Assistant District Attorney, and people are going to take that into account, but if you kill me...''

"I have to kill you, sweetheart. You're the only one who knows all about me and Susie.''

"No, she's not.'' Jamie's knees buckled with relief at the sound of Nathan's deep voice ringing through the dark barn. "I know. And so does an old Indian in Pawhuska.''

Brad's grip on Jamie tightened as he jerked her upright on the ladder. The penlight flared into the darkness from where the voice had come. "Bid-dle?'' Brad shouted. "Stay back! I've got a gun!''

A loud commotion from the stalls broke out, and the horses nickered and whinnied warnings to each other. Suddenly Nathan charged from the darkness, riding bareback on the protesting Sweetie Pie.

Brad fired the gun and missed, but Nathan was upon them, and the horse reared up on hind legs. And before Brad could recover from reeling back-ward, Nathan had kicked the gun from his hand. Jamie twisted herself free in the same instant and jumped from the ladder, moving on hands and knees in the direction the gun had flown. But the narrow beam of the fallen penlight illuminated only the straw on the floor, and Jamie couldn't see the weapon. Out of the corner of her eye she could make out Brad's suit as he clawed his way up the ladder—Jamie couldn't fathom why, unless it was to leap out the hay doors, thirty feet above the ground. Then she saw the hulking figure of Nathan as he threw himself off Sweetie Pie and followed Brad. She flattened herself against a stall gate as the stallion reared again and then moved on. Above her, she heard Brad running across the loft boards, and Nathan's boots pounding the ladder rungs in rapid succession. Then came the cursing, belting, grunting sounds of Nathan and Brad in hand-to-hand combat.

She scrambled to her feet, ran to the penlight, snatched it up and searched for the gun. She saw a glint of metal in the manure gutter and snatched up the weapon. She whirled and pointed the light at the sounds coming from the loft, but the beam only lit a cascade of raining dust and hay. She ran over and climbed the ladder, her injured throat muscles smarting with each pull on the rungs.

When she poked her head over the side of the loft, she caught the fighting men in the beam, but the kicked-up dust and straw kept her from seeing who was winning. Nathan, dressed in lighter denim, was definitely bigger, stronger. He should have crushed Brad by now, but the smaller man's sick desperation seemed to imbue him with power.

"Jamie," Nathan yelled as he ducked Brad's fist, "get back! You'll get hurt!"

But instead, she stepped forward, aimed the gun high and squeezed the trigger. But the warning shot did not stop Brad. He flew into Nathan like one possessed.

Almost immediately the great barn door screeched open. Jamie turned the light to the floor below. A massive shadow moved just beyond the cone of light.

"Robert!" she yelled, waving the tiny beam. "Up here!"

She was gratified to see that Robert could move fast when he wanted to. She aimed the light on the ladder rungs while he ascended in four powerful pulls. She threw herself out of the way as he barreled over the edge of the loft and flung himself at the fighting duo. He yanked Brad off Nathan and bounced him to the loft floor like a rag doll, planting his size-fourteen boot on his throat. Brad fought the pressure like a crazed animal for a second, cursing and choking, before he dissolved into defeated sobs. Jamie got to her feet, rushed forward and aimed the light and the gun between Brad's eyes.

Nathan limped to her side, gasping for air. "Are you okay?" they both said at once.

"I'm fine," Jamie said. "But you're limping. Did he hurt your leg?"

"It's nothing." Nathan took the gun from her, keeping it pointed at Brad. With the other arm he circled her in a strong embrace, and she sank against his side. Nathan turned his head quickly and kissed her hair.

"We could put this vermin out of his misery right now, cousin," Robert announced calmly. He had flipped Brad onto his belly and was mashing his face into the straw. "Let's throw him out to sister moon." He jerked his head toward the hay doors, where moonlight peaked through the cracks.

"If we do—" Nathan was still breathing hard as he held the gun on his wife's murderer "—we're no better than he is."

"You bastard!" Brad spat out. "You don't even have the balls to kill me!"

Nathan's face, a cold mask in the reflected flashlight, showed no emotion as he stared down at Brad.

"You're right," Robert said calmly. "Death is too good for this one."

A moment of silent accord passed between the cousins.

"I'll go down for the rope," Jamie said.

Robert nodded. When she got back, he held the

gun against the back of Brad's head while Nathan tied Brad's hands and feet with the rope. The two men were lowering his bound and squirming body to the barn floor when the sheriff's cruiser lights strobed outside.

Robert steadied one beefy hand on the rope, put fingers to teeth and let out a whistle shrill enough to split eardrums. Instantly alley lights made it as bright as day outside the barn, and the sheriff and two deputies, weapons ready, came bursting through the door that Robert had left ajar.

"Sheriff!" Brad screamed. "They tried to kill me!"

"So you got him?" the sheriff called up to Nathan while he aimed his riot rifle at the man dangling from the rope.

"We got him," Nathan said simply, and let Brad's body fall the few remaining inches to the floor.

One of the deputies rushed forward to take custody of the man.

"Everybody okay?"

"Yep," Robert said.

The sheriff didn't lower his gun. "Then y'all come down that ladder real slow now and explain yourselves."

Robert descended first, but before the two of them started down, Nathan grabbed Jamie again. He held her tightly against his chest, kissed her forehead. "All I could think about was that he might have hurt you," he whispered.

"I'm all right." She pressed her face to his chest because she couldn't say more. He clutched her tighter.

"And that's all that matters to me," Nathan whispered.

CHAPTER SIXTEEN

ROBERT CALLED the next couple of weeks the "strange time of sleepwalking."

Nathan joked that he wouldn't be walking much, asleep or awake, with a bruise the size of a brick on his left thigh. He figured he'd done the damage when he'd leaped off Sweetie Pie. A torn muscle, the doctor said, would take a long time to heal. Everything took a long time to heal, Nathan thought, and he, for one, was sick and tired of healing. He was ready to get on with his life—a life he wanted to share with Jamie Evans.

Jamie's injuries were more superficial, but because her face and neck were too bruised for on-air work, she was given a paid leave of absence from the newsroom. Her parents begged her to come home to Kansas City and she went, but after three days of lonesome long-distance calls, Nathan convinced her to spend her recuperation time at Hart Ranch with him.

They wouldn't be totally alone, he assured her. Robert had moved from Tulsa into the ranch house, and every day Charlie and his wife, Martha, drove over. Charlie did extra chores while Nathan's leg was healing, and Martha spent the day cooking soothing buttery foods like rich beef stew, barbecued chicken, fried okra and cinnamon rolls.

Jamie tried to be enthusiastic about the "wonders" of ranch life because she knew how important the place was to Nathan. But she was still terrified of the horses, discovered that most of the routine chores were genuinely unpleasant, and found the mere smell of wild fowl cooking enough to make her retch.

And she found the isolation almost more than she could bear. Her only consolation, besides the physical closeness of Nathan—was Robert's one-eyed mastiff, Bear. The shaggy old dog liked to follow Jamie around every day when she pulled on high boots and tramped through the fresh snow, now more than a foot deep. Slowly, on those long cold walks, Jamie began to feel a kinship with this land, a love of these vast Osage Hills.

Even so, by the beginning of the second week, she was checking in with Dave a couple of times a day. Nathan was passing through the kitchen about sundown, and he heard her out on the veranda talking on her cell phone, laughing at the office gossip with her cameraman. He realized she missed her work. He had much to say to this woman, and his time was growing short.

That night it snowed again, and he found Jamie

and Robert slumped on the leather couch before the massive fireplace with old black-and-white photos of the Hart family spread on the marble coffee table before them. Jamie was holding the one of Black Wing that looked eerily like Nathan. Nathan came up behind the couch and studied it over her shoulder. "He looks like an old Buddha wrapped in an Indian blanket, doesn't he?"

Jamie examined the deep-set eyes, the broad straight nose, the granite-hard square jaw. "He looks like you, Nathan Biddle."

Nathan said nothing, thinking that perhaps now the time was right.

He rounded the couch and squatted before the fire, poking at the logs.

"Robert, you look sleepy."

Robert, who actually looked perfectly alert, smiled shyly and laid the photograph he'd planned to show Jamie next on the table. "Cousin, I believe you're right. Good night, Jamie." He thumped up the stairs.

"What was that—" Jamie started.

"We haven't really talked," Nathan interrupted. He was still on his haunches, facing the fire.

"About what?" Jamie asked softly.

"All of it. Susie. Her death. Alexander."

"Are you ready to talk about it?"

"Only with you."

"Okay. We'll talk."

"What did Brad tell you that night?"

"Lies, Nathan. Terrible lies. He was desperate. I think what he finally told the police is the true story."

"That he and Susie went to the same private school as kids, and that she started turning to him when she became upset with me, so he assumed they were in love."

"He's a sick man."

"It still hurts that she kept all those relationships a secret from me. I never knew…!"

"Like Hunter told you, those relationships were one-sided. They meant nothing to her. Maybe Susie was a bit foolish to confide in Brad later, but she wasn't a bad person. I doubt she ever even saw Brad as a real man. You know that."

When he didn't turn to look at her, she went on, hoping to bring him some kind of peace with her words. "But I think he was truly obsessed with her. That old footage where he's in the background? You can tell by looking closely that Susie was bothered when she saw him there. She had eyes only for you, Nathan."

"You're being awfully generous to the first wife."

The *first* wife? Jamie couldn't stop herself from thinking his wording had significance. Maybe it was unintentional, but just the thought of him having *another* wife—*her*—made her heart beat faster.

"I can afford to be generous," she managed to answer calmly, "now that I know how you feel about me."

"Yes. How I feel about you. That's what I really want to talk about."

Nathan stood, but instead of coming to her, he crossed the room to the massive picture window where he'd seen his first vision.

Robert had discovered, through the shaman, that in the old days people had called the spot where Susie died Weeping Faces Cliff.

An involuntary shudder passed through Jamie as she wondered what he was thinking, what he was seeing. Nathan's...gift was apparently real. Would the visions keep coming now that the threat was behind them? she wondered. It didn't matter whether they did or they didn't. He was a changed man. Now, she knew, in his heart he *believed*. And always would.

As if he could read her mind, Nathan said, "Jamie, you know when Robert and I went to see that old guy who claimed to be a shaman?"

"Mr. Elliott?"

"Yeah. Remember how I told you the stuff he said was nothing but a bunch of Indian mumbo-jumbo?"

"I remember." Jamie smiled. How could she ever forget that night?

"Well, it turns out that some of what he said kind of...kind of makes sense."

"Oh?" Jamie chose not to insert any I-told-you-so's into this important conversation.

"Yeah." He stood looking out at the snow falling softly in the moonlight. "He said that when the snow came, it would cover my past and I could make new tracks."

Jamie's heart started to pound as he reached into his hip pocket and slowly withdrew a piece of tattered paper. "It's funny how it all comes together, isn't it?" he said as he slowly unfolded it.

"There was actually a time when I thought true love was going to be a once-in-a-lifetime deal for me, and then..." His voice grew soft as he stood there with the paper in his hand, looking more vulnerable, more masculine, more beautiful than he ever had. "Jamie, what I'm trying to say is..."

She couldn't even nod.

He looked out at the dark hills again. "I need you to understand the true meaning of this ranch for me. I want you to understand who those people are." He aimed the paper at the photographs on the table. "I want you to understand my Osage heritage. Because I want...I want us to live together here as husband and wife."

Jamie's breath caught. She had known this was coming, but not so soon. She wanted to be with Nathan with her whole heart, but as she tried to answer him, she found her throat so dry she couldn't speak. How would they ever work this out? Already she was chomping at the bit to get back on the air. And Nathan wasn't the kind of man to wait forever for his answer once the question was asked. "Oh, Nathan," she finally breathed.

He turned to her, and after looking into her eyes for a long time, crossed the room and knelt beside the couch, taking her hands gently in his large ones.

She felt tears stinging at her eyes as she tried to find the words to tell him how much she loved him, but that she wouldn't—couldn't—give up her career. "Marriage is such a big step," she whispered, "and there's so much we still need to discuss."

"Such as?" He got off his knee and sat beside her on the couch.

"Such as...whether or not to have children."

He narrowed his eyes at her, sensing her evasion. "You want some kids?"

"Of course."

"No problem. I'll do my part to make that happen."

Jamie had to smile. "Nathan, I'm serious."

"I am, too. I love kids. Look, Jamie, all I'm saying is, we know each other in all the ways that count—the ways of the heart."

"Now you sound like an Indian." Jamie smiled.

"I *am* an Indian."

"And I *am* a television reporter. That's my dream—my identity. I told you that."

Suddenly he looked as if he understood her hesitation. He closed his eyes and raised her knuckles to his lips, kissing them tenderly. "I don't want to change that."

"You don't? Then how am I supposed to live out on this ranch and chase down stories for Channel Six?"

Unable to answer that question, Nathan lowered his head.

"Nathan, we have to be honest here. I love you. You know that. I've never loved anyone besides you, and I probably never will. But I can't stop being a reporter. It's what I'm meant to do, the same way you feel that this ranch is what you're meant to do." She laced her fingers in his and squeezed. "If I asked you to give up the ranch, you wouldn't be the man I fell in love with, and if you asked me to give up my career, I wouldn't be the same woman you've come to love. Hell, I'm about to lose my mind out here and I've only been here a week." She put her forehead against his in frustration.

After a few moments Nathan jerked his head up. "Wow," he breathed. His eyes sparked with excitement.

"What?" Jamie said, hoping he had an answer to their dilemma.

"It just hit me. The old man, the shaman, he said I would always walk in two worlds. I thought he was talking about my being part white and part Osage. That would have been an easy prediction. All people of Native American heritage walk in two worlds. But maybe he was talking about us, about this ranch and Tulsa."

"And?"

"Don't you see? I always swore I'd never go back to the life I had in Tulsa, but I wouldn't be going back to that life at all. I'd be going to a new life—with *you*."

"Nathan, do you mean you'd—?"

"I mean, we can make this work. Why couldn't we come to the ranch for weekends, holidays, or whenever we felt like it? Or I could deed the whole thing to Robert, sell the horses to Charlie and Martha, and we could just visit the place occasionally."

"I couldn't ask you to do that."

"Why not?"

"Because it's your life! And I'm starting to get used to this ranch, too, and maybe even the horses—from a healthy distance. I don't want you to give all that up for me. But I'm not ready to give up my life in Tulsa, either. Not yet. I worked too hard for it."

"Then you can keep your place and I'll keep my horses, and you can come out here on weekends and we can...work on those kids." He wrapped his arms around her and gave her a playful peck on the nose. "Whaddaya think?"

She closed her eyes, thinking of all he'd just offered to give up for her. And suddenly she realized it didn't matter where they lived or what they did, because if they were going to be together, they would have to both be flexible as they found a unique way to blend their two worlds. "Oh, Nathan, I think I'm going to have to find a way to walk those two worlds with you."

"Thank you," he said hoarsely as he brought his warm urgent mouth to hers.

The kiss, long and deep and passionate, sealed their commitment.

When at last they pulled apart, Jamie glanced at the small piece of paper, which Nathan had discarded on top of the photographs when he'd come to kneel before her. "What is that?"

"Something I've been saving for you." Nathan reached for the paper. "A poem."

"A poem?"

"Yeah. It's...an Osage poem, actually."

"Osage? One of Robert's reclaimed ones? Who wrote this one? A chief? A shaman?"

"No." Nathan looked into her eyes as he drew a deep breath. "I did."

Jamie placed her fingers on her lips. "You wrote a poem for me?"

Nathan nodded.

"With all that's happened, when did you ever find the time?"

"It came to me. The first time I had a dream about you."

"Oh, God." She felt breathless. No one had ever written a poem for her.

"Close your eyes," he said.

She did. And then she heard the paper rustle as he unfolded it. He cleared his throat and in his low resonant voice read:

Your heart beats in the heart of my dreams,
Calling me from a dark winter sleep.
Come to me, oh most beautiful of women.
Come to the one who is calling you,
Come to the heart of the Osage.

HARLEQUIN *Super*ROMANCE

**To celebrate the
1000th Superromance book
We're presenting you with 3 books
from 3 of your favorite authors in**

All Summer Long

Home, Hearth and Haley
by **Muriel Jensen**

Meet the men and women of Muriel's
upcoming **Men of Maple Hill** trilogy

Daddy's Girl
by **Judith Arnold**

Another **Daddy School** story!

Temperature Rising
by **Bobby Hutchinson**

Life and love at St. Joe's Hospital are as feverish
as ever in this **Emergency!** story

On sale July 2001
Available wherever Harlequin books are sold.

HARLEQUIN®
Makes any time special ®

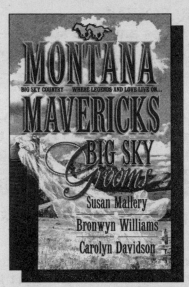

DON'T MISS OUT!

MONTANA MAVERICKS: BIG SKY GROOMS
Three brand-new historical stories about the Kincaids, Montana's most popular family

RETURN TO WHITEHORN, MONTANA—
WHERE LEGENDS ARE BEGUN AND
LOVE LASTS FOREVER BENEATH THE BIG SKY....

Available in August 2001

Visit us at www.eHarlequin.com

PHBSGR

In August 2001
New York Times bestselling author

HEATHER GRAHAM

joins

DALLAS SCHULZE

&

Elda Minger

in

TAKE5

Volume 3

These five heartwarming love
stories are quick reads, great escapes
and guarantee five times the joy.

HARLEQUIN *Super*ROMANCE®

CREATURE COMFORT

A heartwarming new series by

Carolyn McSparren

**Creature Comfort, the largest veterinary
clinic in Tennessee, treats animals of all
sizes—horses and cattle as well as family
pets. Meet the patients—and their owners.
And share the laughter and the tears with
the men and women who love and care
for all creatures great and small.**

#996 THE MONEY MAN
(July 2001)

#1011 THE PAYBACK MAN
(September 2001)

*Look for these Harlequin Superromance titles
coming soon to your favorite retail outlet.*

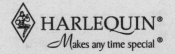

HARLEQUIN®
Makes any time special ®